CW01499476

PREFACE

I saw him and I froze.

Why after all these years was he here?

How did he find me?

What to do?

What to say?

All I could do was stand there frozen just like the first time. It seems I have always been like this frozen in time.

Time stood still.

My soul froze.

So many questions.

How could it be?

How did the world return him to me?

Is he a dream?

Is it real?

Am I?

The Boy

Lindsay

Melissa

DEDICATION

I dedicate this book to God because although this book talks about love and soulmates I believe everyone has a true love, the one that never fails is God's love. I just love to imagine and create different love stories because I am a dreamer at heart. My soulmates here on earth would be my children because in my life they are the ones that make the world turn. So, Kevin, Alex and Kaitlin this book is also dedicated to you three. I love you. 💕

ACKNOWLEDGMENTS

I must acknowledge the little things in life that we sometimes don't see or value. A friendly face, a reassuring word and sometimes even a smile or hello. We never know when a small act of kindness will make a change in someone's day. For those little things in life which sometimes was just what I needed to get through dark, cloudy days. To those of you out there just be nice it doesn't cost anything and it makes you look more beautiful than all the makeup in the world. A good soul is a worthier treasure than all the physical beauty and the riches in the whole world so next time you meet a stranger or two in the street simply take a minute look up and smile.

1 THE BEGINNING

I remember everything from that day. I was wearing a simple white summer dress, my hair in a high ponytail. I remember the smells of that morning. That morning dew smell after a light rain. I was happy. I was in high school living a "normal" teenage life. Nothing particular or special that day (or so I thought). That day that I could not even imagine how much my life would change. My world was about to be flipped upside down.

I opened my front door ready to walk to school, which was only two blocks away. I looked up and there HE was. Was he a vision? He was standing across the street. He was so handsome. Blonde, blue eyed boy. Blue jeans and a simple white t-shirt. He was looking straight at me. It was not that he was staring at me, but that it felt he saw right to the depths of my soul. I felt in a way naked. Naked in the sense that I felt he could see all the way to my deepest root of what was I. He was seeing right to the core of me. His eyes blue like the sky, his hair waving in the breeze.

Tell me what would you do if someone looked at you like that. A piercing look that chilled your bones but warmed your heart. I thought to myself who the heck was he and why was he here? But most of all I felt myself thinking and feeling please don't leave. It seems that this moment lasted a really long time when in fact it was probably a matter of seconds. This moment was stamped into my memory forever.

This is the moment that I started to live. Every sense in my body was awakened. I opened my eyes for the first time to the wonders of the world and to the wonder of the feeling of love. It is so weird how one simple instance in time can change and cause a ripple on your whole existence or even possibly change your purpose and reason for being! I did not know what to do. Should I say hi? Should I look away? I was so drawn to him. He was stunning. The only way to explain it is that it felt like a magnet. Impossible to discard or ignore. Impossible to look away even if I tried. There we stood two humans in the middle of this planet so drawn to each other, looking at each other for the first time and feeling newly discovered emotions of what must be what they call love at first sight.

Finally, after what seemed to me hours but was actually just a few seconds he smiled. Oh, my goodness he smiled! All of a sudden the sun shone a little bit brighter. His smile was radiant. He just made my soul tremble. His smile had so much power over me I felt I could literally melt right into a puddle like the wicked witch of the West in the land of Oz. Or was it the wicked witch of the East? His smile was everything to me at that moment.

It is hard to put into words what his smile did to me. If I could bottle up the feelings he caused it would be so electrifying the bottle would burst. It was like fireworks. I probably stood there just like a complete idiot for I don't know how long. What was happening? Did he cast a spell on me? He then disappeared. Just like that... poof he was gone. I looked all around and there was no sign of him anywhere. The world got a little dimmer again.

My heart sunk to my stomach. My breath returned to my lungs. I could not believe this just happened. Was I day-dreaming all of it? Am I crazy? My heart was pounding like a racing horse and it was ready to win the race it was going so fast. There are moments in life that are so incredible you think you just envisioned them. There are not many. They will pass you by if you don't stop and take notice. If you blink you might even miss one. It felt so strong yet it was really nothing, nothing but a stare and a smile. Nothing so out of the ordinary, right?

This exact moment changed me I just did not know how much it had impacted me back then. It moved my thoughts. My emotions felt sparked. How? I had no idea that it was just the start. This boy, whose name I did not even know, with one look left an imprint in me. How was this possible? Did I go insane? Did this really just happen? I had no words. I had never felt anything like this before.

Was this what people called love at first sight? I knew deep inside of me it was much more than that. More intense, deeper than that emotion people call love. I actually saw my soulmate. A piece of my soul if you can understand that! Our souls were somehow a part of each other's. Somehow, someway I felt a connection to him. I did not understand any of it but all I knew is that I had to see him. Maybe even say hi next time! This was something my soul knew it had to do. I had never believed in this sort of thing but now at this exact moment my whole world had been flipped upside down and new doors that I did not even know existed opened up and where ready for me to open them and walk right through.

He consumed my thoughts the rest of the day and every day for weeks. All I knew is that I had to see him again. I looked for him everywhere. I began to look for him even in the shadows. It was like a hunger. I hungered for this boy. My mind, my body was calling for him.

The days passed and I could not concentrate on school, home life or anything People would normally describe me as an outgoing type of girl. You could usually find me giggling with my friends at school or joking around with my family at home. Since I saw the boy I was numb. All I could do was think of him. I seemed to be floating everywhere like a ghost. The days passed and they didn't faze me. All I wanted was to see the boy again. I actually ached. Life was on pause.

What the heck happened to me? How much control could I lose to a stranger? This was in no way normal but who could I tell? Who would believe me without laughing at me or thinking that I went completely crazy? I was so confused and kind of angry for allowing someone to have so much power over me, especially if it was an unknown stranger who I had never set eyes on.

For all I knew he could be a fugitive or even a thief. I decided that he was a thief. He had stolen my heart. Somehow and without permission he took off with it and left me here without even a word. I know it sounds corny but I became "that" girl. Yet I knew all of this was meant to be. I just knew it was meant to happen. In a way, it even felt natural. What was unnatural was for him to just leave like that.

Each day I woke up and opened the door getting ready to face the world and hoping, wishing, praying to come face to face with HIM once again. Not really knowing what I would do if it did happen. Last time I could not even move. Would I be able to even say hi? Would I be able to even breath!

My childish thoughts told me to run, grab him and never let him go. Yeah right! How would that look! This is my natural wants and basic instincts talking of course. The feelings and thoughts we have that are raw until society's rules, that are instilled in us since the time we were born, take over and then we feel ashamed, silly or just wrong. Society breaks us.

The days kept rolling by and when I least expected I opened the door and there he was. Just as clear as daylight. He stood there looking my way again. He was the most beautiful boy I had ever seen. I definitely knew he was not from around here. Again, he took my breath away.

I felt like I was floating on air. I felt like in a dreamlike state, a trance. What was this? He hypnotized me. But this time it went a little differently than last time.

"Hi." He said. My tongue could not move. It felt heavy. Words could not be assembled. My brain turned to a big pile of mush. Did I forget how to speak? Again, I asked myself what was this?

"Hi." He repeated.
"Oh, hello." I finally spitted out.
"I'm Jax."
Silence.

Oh, my gosh, the jitters in my stomach were not like butterflies, they were more like bats. He was actually speaking to me! This boy, this blonde, blue eyed boy was talking to me! I was acting like a boy had never spoke to me before. I started to feel somewhat embarrassed because it was as if I did not know how to behave. I was sixteen years old and not a child any more. What was he going to think!

2 JAX

When his words came out I do not exaggerate when I say they sounded like when the rivers run or when waves crash on the shore at the beach. The sound of his voice comforted my soul like it was being stroked with the softest piece of cloud from heaven. Jax. His name was Jax was all my brain could register. As if Jax was the greatest thing since peanut butter and jelly. Jax. Jax. Jax. My heart could not stop beating.

"My name is Katherine, Kate for short" I finally responded.

"I know." He answered

"You know?"

How could he possibly know?

"Yeah, I know. I have traveled from far away searching for you. You are Kate. I am Jax. You are my other half."

He simply stated like that was the most normal thing to say to a girl he just met. Probably a pick-up line. I must say it was a good one too since it made me even more curious to keep talking to him. In reality this boy could get away with telling me the moon was made out of cheese and I would believe him. Just with his smile alone....

"Ohhh kayyy...!?"

What do I say to that? How do I respond? I did not care if it was a cheesy pick up line. I was drawn to him. I was happy it was directed towards me. I was happy he was even here.

"Katherine Peters, you love rocky road ice cream, you draw really good, you have a scar on your knee that you got from roller skating when you were little and you hate mustard."

"What! How do you know? Are you a hacker, stalker, creeper?"

I should have felt creeped out that he was turning out to be a complete weirdo and mysterious guy who knew too much. Instead I felt confused, curious and amazingly even more drawn in.

I wanted to know how he could possibly take time to research me. Why me? Out of anyone in the world he was talking to me or should I say stalking me? Should I feel honored he picked me, could he possibly be attracted to me? Questions and more questions.

"No, I told you, you are my soulmate."

Again, he spoke like that was so natural to say to a person you just met! What to make of this?

"Ok, so you have researched me out. Cool. You probably got on my Facebook and looked me up, there is so much information out there. Where do you live? Where did you come from I mean?"

I also secretly felt like adding on "and please don't ever leave."

"I came from a place that is out of this world, I live there. I needed to find you. I needed for you to know me. We are finally together. The bond is sealed. Once you and I looked into each other's eyes we sealed our bond. Didn't you feel it when you saw me the other day? "

"I definitely felt something. I still don't understand it. Are you playing with me? Is this a joke? What is happening?"

Our bond? Sealed? Huh? What was happening here? Was I being punked? Was this all a prank??? I started to think which of my friends would do something like this to me. I looked and looked around to see if I could spot any hidden cameras. Nothing. Then again how could they anticipate me falling for someone instantly. That right there shows they could never plan this out especially as hard as I fell for this boy. I felt like I was on a TV show. Instead of having clarity I felt more confused than before.

"This is going to take me some time to explain. How about I give you some time to soak some of this in and I will meet with you later?"

What! Later! No, every cell of my body did not want later. I did not want him to walk away.

"Later? When, later?" I said too quickly.

I needed to know exactly when and where right now. I think I missed him even before he had even left! My boy was about to leave, again.

"Don't worry, I will find you. If I found you worlds away I think I can find you anywhere." He laughed

How could he laugh! This felt so serious to me. How could this feel so serious? I just met the guy. How could he become so important to me so fast and so much? It felt like he was like my oxygen. I needed him. My skin urged for him to be near. My heart clicked with his. We probably even had our heartbeats in sync. Was this love? Was this a dream, a fantasy?

"Let me give you my cell phone number so you can text me."

"No, I don't need it."

"Do you have that information too?" I joked.

"No, I just don't need it. Relax, I will find you always, no matter where you go I will find you. I really have to let you go though. You have a family and a life to go to and I don't mean to disrupt it. I actually was not meant to seek you till later in life. I am early. Too early, not sure if that was a mistake. Please, trust me when I say we will meet again very soon. I look forward to it my dear."

And just like that he left. Gone.

I was flabbergasted. My dear? I was his dear? Whaaat!!????

He left and I had to admit I needed time to think. It felt like just in an instant my life was different. My life all of a sudden shifted. What I use to feel was important was not so much anymore. What I was going to wear to school the next day or who I was going to prom with were issues that meant everything to me just a few days ago and now seemed so distant and so trivial. He was important. He was everything to me now.

I was acting like a silly schoolgirl. Oh, my God I wasn't *acting* like a silly school girl I actually *was* a silly schoolgirl. Oh, my goodness, I did just turn into "that" girl? The girl who is mushy mushy with a guy. I had never been like this before. Yes, I had boyfriends, actually just one boyfriend before but it wasn't like this at all.

I again went to my sulky, quiet mood. My parents asked me what was wrong with me. I could see their worried looks on their faces. I was not the same girl. I just told them it was just nerves from the finals coming up. They nodded and accepted that answer. I mean what could I tell them?

Nothing significant had happened except that I met a boy, a complete stranger. I only spoke to him once and now here I was. Sulking and waiting. As the days passed I tried to focus on my schoolwork. I even tried to pretend to be interested in what my friends and I would normally be excited about. They had noticed a change in me. They also asked if I was okay. I just smiled, nodded and tried to sound enthusiastic about the dances that were coming up and most importantly graduation. Those were big deals to my peers, and they were a big deal to me too until recently.

As the days passed my school began to prepare for graduation, prom and all the typical end of the year senior activities. I tried my best to have fun with it. My grades had always been pretty good. I knew I would graduate with no problem. Now my problem was just getting through the days. Prom was coming, should I even go? I wanted to go with Jax. Only Jax. Nothing would ever be the same.

It was as if my life could only go on with Jax in it. I wondered when would be the next time that he would show up. It was exciting to think that it would most likely be different next time. I hoped that he would spend more time with me and that we could actually get to talk longer. I had so many questions.

Sometimes people talk about a turning point in their lives where they can pinpoint exactly when they feel their lives changed. Usually they are events like a wedding, divorce, birth of a child you know, significant events. For me it would be the day I saw Jax for the first time. Instantly in that same second I saw him I felt my world freeze. From then on everything was different.

It was as if I was living a life half asleep and now all of a sudden I woke up. My senses were more alert, more aware, more alive. I saw everything differently, the colors of the world were now brighter, smells were more intense and it was also like now I had a new sense. This sense is not easy to describe or even explain. It is like a feeling of just being, of existing. A sense of deep, true love? When I use the word love I use it because that is the closest word to describe this feeling that had overtaken my world.

Is this what love was? Is this what others felt? Something inside of me told me that this was something different from love. Stronger even. Every pore in my body was screaming how it was connected to Jax. This was not love, this was not lust or even want. It was like my body and soul were literally made to be with Jax.

He had mentioned that we were soulmates. Did that really exist? It made sense to me. It had to be. Hmmm….Soul-mates, I liked the sound of that. If I could have him as a soulmate I would not complain. He was the most perfect boy I had ever met in my life. None of the boys at school compared to him. I have heard that term before but never really paid any attention to it. Jax was definitely my soulmate. No doubts at all in my mind about that.

Without knowing anything about him I just knew. It was just like how I knew the sky is blue and the grass is green. Just like I also knew birds fly and fish swim. Jax was a part of me. Period. No discussion, no having to need proof. He was my soulmate and that was more real than anything. I just needed to know what happens now? I found my soul-mate, or he actually found me. He vanished and now my life could not continue without him, it made absolutely no sense at all.

3 THE MEETING

I was walking to meet up with my friends when all of a sudden I felt a knot in my stomach. I felt a chill down my spine and I knew. I turned around by instinct and there he was. The boy. My boy. My soulmate. My Jax. Yes, mine. I felt he was mine already. I cannot even describe the joy I felt. It was like what a child feels when they wake up on Christmas morning. That excitement and happiness that is just pure and you don't want it to go away.

"Hi!" I said maybe too cheerfully.

"Hi, my sweet Kate. Finally, can we go for coffee, sit and chat for a while?" Like I would say no. I felt like jumping up and down like a cheerleader.

"Yeah, of course."

My eyes could not get enough of his gorgeous, perfect face. Walking next to him I smelled him and he smelled soooo good. I could not keep my eyes from him. I wanted to memorize every detail about him. I felt like the luckiest girl in the universe. Like I had won the lottery and I was still in shock. He could be walking with anyone and here he was next to me! He chose me! I was giddy.

All of a sudden, he stretched out his arm and held my hand. Our first touch. I felt a shock of electricity run through all the nerves of my body. All my mind was saying was Oh My God! His touch. Him holding my hand, something as simple as that and I felt like I was floating. He looked at me and smiled. I smiled back.

"Is this ok?" He asked.

"Sure." I mumbled. It was more than ok!

"You are so warm."

His voice was sweet, gentle, and charming. That was the word for him, charming. My prince charming. He did not come in a white horse but he could have come to me barefoot and in scrubs and he still would be my prince Charming. His blue eyes are like the color of the sky. His silky blonde hair blowing in the wind was like a prince from one of the Disney movies. And me? I was just a typical, average girl. Plain Kate. Not ugly but not spectacular either. That gave me a sharp pain all of a sudden. Why me? How come he chose me?

We walked in silence all the way to the coffee shop. I wanted to say a thousand things but nothing came out. Us walking hand in hand in silence when we had so much to talk about was just the best feeling in the world. It felt like it was a normal thing to be doing. We walked like we had been dating for years. Like an old married couple. I felt nervous but at the same time comfortable, safe, loved.

We walked in and like a gentlemen, he pulled out my chair for me. I sat down. He sat and just looked deep into my eyes. I had never had anyone look at me like that before. That look of his. He was looking at me in that way again. I had no secrets from him, he saw me for who I was. He could see the girl that I was without me having to tell him. I knew this somehow or at least that is how I felt. I was frozen again. No words. I could not even move. I wondered if this was normal.

"Hi, may I take your order?" A waitress came by and popped our bubble.

"Sure, I will have coffee and a grilled cheese please." Jax quickly ordered and looked at me waiting for me to order. "and you darling?"

Darling... he called me darling.

"I will have coffee and a bagel with cream cheese please. "

The waitress grabbed the menus and walked away. I noticed how she looked at Jax. She clearly noticed how good looking he was and it made me jealous. Urghhh. I was not surprised because of how cute he was he must get these looks everywhere. I actually care. Wow.

"My darling, where to begin. I have so much to tell you. There is so much for you to know. I sit here and all I want to do is grab you, hold you and kiss you but you need to know who I am and most of all who WE are."

I would have not been mad with him with the grabbing and holding me part but I did need to know and wanted to know everything. I needed to understand what was going on with me. Was it mind control because that was exactly what if felt like.

"Yes, I want to know who you are and why I feel like this with you." I knew that he understood what "this" was. "How come you hypnotize me? How come I feel so strongly for you if I don't even know you? Who are you, where did you come from and why me? "

" First of all, I want to warn you that there are things that will be difficult for you to understand at first. I will be telling you some things that may seem really hard to believe. I am not crazy or a psycho or a stalker or anything like that. At first you might not believe but I ask that you take time. I will try to go as slow as I can even though I wish I could just fast forward and just be able to love you. Because I do. I love you but here I go getting ahead of myself. I apologize, let me slow down a bit."

Love? Did he say he loves me!!! OMG. He loves me. I love him too. OMG I love him!

"Jax, the more you talk the less I understand. How can you love me? How come I feel I love you too? I don't know you, you don't love me. How is this possible? "

His face glowed a little when I said I loved him too. He was happy to hear these words from my mouth. His face seemed sincere. He did not look like he was faking it at all. This made me feel really nice inside. I had never, ever said those three words to anyone before except of course my parents. It felt very good saying it to Jax. The surprising part is that it felt like I had always been saying it to him. It did not feel like it was the first time. The words just rolled out of my tongue and there they were, without concern, shame or regret.

The waitress came back. She brought our food. The whole time not taking her eyes off Jax. That exasperated me so much. She smiled at him the whole time and I just wanted her to hurry up and leave us alone. I wanted to be alone. I did not want to share him not even with a few minutes with the waitress! I wondered how I have become so protective and possessive. That just was not my personality at all.

"There is an explanation for everything. I just don't know how to say it without sounding crazy. Ok here goes. Kate, the reason we love each other is that we are soulmates. That I told you already. You and I are meant to be together always. When our souls are together we fit, we are connected, we are complete. When they are apart something is always missing, nothing is the same. There are many souls that have soulmates and some are lucky to find them and some are not so lucky. I was very, very lucky more than you know. You see with us there is something different compared to the average couple. We are unique. When soulmates are matched they are placed in the universe in specific locations and depending on the peoples decisions and the paths they chose in life it either leads them together or not. With us there was a little mistake made. No, not little, let me rephrase that, a HUGE mistake was made"

"A mistake? " I freaked out. No, this could not be a mistake, this felt perfect. "What kind of mistake?"

"Yes, a mistake that we were placed too far apart. Farther than any soulmate has been ever placed, ever. You see, sometimes soulmates are placed on one side of the world from the other. You and I were placed on the other side of the universe from each other."

"What you are telling me is that you came from the other side of the universe? From another planet? Are you an astronaut?" I was really confused now.

"No, I am what you call an alien."

4 MYTHICAL REALITY

"So, you come from another country is what you mean right?" I asked, but somehow I did not think this is what he meant.

"No, another universe."

"You, mean another social scale like you walk in a different social circle than me?"

"No another universe" He was serious when he talked. He was not kidding.

Oh God! What the heck was he talking about? Another universe? I was in a movie. This must be a hidden camera show and everyone must be laughing so hard at me. Here I am like an idiot going along with this and actually believing it or wanting to believe it. I got a little irritated and upset.

"Look, I know I am young and look innocent but I know I am not going to let you just make fun of me."

"No, sweetheart I really am from another place far, far away. Maybe I should have not started with this. Maybe it's too soon and maybe I should leave."

No, don't leave I wanted to scream. No, I don't want this to end. Should I go along with it? My heart raced. I just knew that I did not care what he told me I just could not let him leave. Not yet. I needed more time with him.

"No, please don't go. Please tell me more. I don't understand and I want to, please don't be mad. Don't leave."

"Are you sure? Are you really sure you are ready?"

How could I answer that? Could anyone be ready for something like this? Did this really happen to people? Was I crazy to go along with this? All I could do is do anything to make him not go away so I decided to keep listening. See what happened. It was like I was living a fantasy. I was dreaming but I was awake. Dreaming and I did not want to wake up. Yes, I would go along with it. Pretend this was a movie and I was the princess and he was my prince. My prince. My boy.

"Where I come from is very different in some ways and alike in other ways. We are very similar in that we are also humans and that God created us as well. We feel, we eat, we breath in all of that we are the same. We are made of skin and bones. We get sick, we get hurt, we live, we die. My planet is called Avian"

Then he grabbed my hand and placed it on his heart.

"Feel. My heart beating just as hard as yours."

I felt his muscles in his chest and I felt his heart. His touch. His touch that made me feel excited like I have never felt before. Touching him validated that he existed, that he was actually here, with me. He was real. His heart was racing just like mine was.

During all this conversation, we hardly touched our food. Our coffee was done. At this moment, the waitress came back. Again, all googly-eyed for Jax. Made me just want to slap her. He took money from his wallet, paid and then held out his hand for me to take it. I was more than willing to hold his hand. We walked out. Where are we off to? I just did not want him to stop holding my hand.

"Can we go to the park? I believe we have more to discuss. If you wish that is. Or if you rather we can finish this conversation another day. I just want to go at your pace. I know it is a lot to take in."

"No way, let's go to the park. I have a million more questions than I did in the beginning! I want to know, I want you to tell me all about you and where you come from. Please, I need to know more. I want to believe and understand you."

"Ok, my darling let's go."

He held my hand strongly as if he was to let go he would lose me or something. His eyes looked forward and every few minutes I could see him looking at me from the corner of his eyes. He walked calmly. I couldn't feel prouder to be walking hand in hand with him. Could a guy like him really be interested in me? How could this be? How could I be so lucky? My brain still had not registered all of what was happening.

"Am I truly your darling? Are you sure you picked the right girl?" I asked him.

"You are so much more than my darling. You are my everything. You mean so much to me that I left my home, traveled for so long, risked everything, to be here with you. To be united finally. You and I together like it was supposed to be from the start. You are my light. Without you I had been living in darkness. Never have I been more sure of any decision I have ever made in all of my life. I am so sure and I know you know it too. As crazy as all this must be for you I know you feel as strongly as I do for the reason that we are meant to be like this. Together, hand in hand."

To hear those words. To hear them just from a normal girlfriend/boyfriend relationship must feel so wonderful. To hear them from him, from my Jax, from my soulmate Jax, feels incredible. There are no words for what I was feeling.

We finally made it to a nearby park, found a picnic table and sat next to each other. We were facing each other, electricity was what was going on between us. Sparks of .... Sparks of an invisible energy so strong that it was a miracle it could not be seen. So, this was the chemistry I always heard about! I must have miss something in class! We must be glowing. I felt just like that. Like we were in some magical bubble and it was glowing like a star.

"Jax, before you start. Just tell me one thing. Is this all a dream? Am I crazy?" Jax laughed a little. He was amused by me I guess.

"No, not at all. This is our destiny."

"Let me try and explain again I will go as slow as I can. It's hard because I know there is a lot to say. In your world, your people have the bible. Some believe in it some don't. Fact is it is mostly true. God did create your universe and everything in it. What it doesn't say is that he created so many other universes, with other worlds, with other living creatures. Some worlds know about each other and some are still primitive like yours is. We are advanced because we were created before you and God made different rules in our world. Our technology is advanced. We can communicate with angels and we can travel to other worlds. We worship God and we don't have the devil roaming our planet. So, you see a little different."

"A little, a lot!!! I have no words. Tell me more... go on..."

Wow, I was so hungry to know more. The more he spoke the more interested I was in him and in everything he had to say. He talked and talked about his planet Avian. It seemed amazing. The more he spoke the more fascinated I became.

"Okay, so like I said we were created as soulmates but I was put in my planet, Avian and you on earth. Somehow, we were not sent to the same planet, which never happens. I am not sure if this was part of the plan or not but I could not live any longer without you so I broke some rules at home. I left without permission and have been searching for you in your world for some time now. Normally when we travel there is a procedure. When we travel to another planet it is for a reason like to help others, study your planet and contribute to it. We are not allowed to go for personal reasons or out of selfishness. I acted selfish and left without seeking approval first. I am at risk right now of being found and sent immediately back. If I do I will have to face serious consequences. This is my biggest fear. I can't lose you."

No, I can't lose him. He can't be taken away.

"I can't lose you when I just found you! Don't let them, I can't be without you ever again. We have to be together. I need you" I cried out.

I know I probably, no, not probably, for sure, sounded like a little stupid and desperate person. I was in high school after all. I was just a teenager. A teenager that was faced with the biggest fear of losing someone she just found out she loved with all her heart and soul. A teenager who found her first true love. They say you never forget your first love and if this is why know I understand completely.

"People from my planet are probably looking for me right now as I speak. Kate, I just need you to believe me. My intentions are pure. Give me your hand."

Our hands touched. The energy just by our hands touching was incredible. I closed my eyes and just concentrated on what I was feeling. I felt like I belonged to something, to him. For the first time in my life I felt satisfied. I felt my heart completely full. This is so hard to explain. It's like you no longer long for anything in life. Like feeling accomplished, alive, beautiful, loved and satisfied all at once. My reason for existing was to be with Jax.

"Do you see, Kate?" He asked me. "Do you feel what I am talking about? It is easier to feel than to explain. You have to see with your heart. Listen to what it is telling you. "

He then put his hand down but kept holding my hand in his.

"We belong to each other. Do you understand?"
"Yeah, I think I do!"

"When we are together the world is a beautiful place to live. When we are a part we feel something is always missing. We never feel satisfied or complete. That is the way it works. Some people try to find what is missing and throw themselves into work or hobbies. Other people into church, others into drugs and so on. Everyone is trying to find that missing link. Some will find it and some wont. I found you, now we have to fight for us. We are together right now but tomorrow we don't know what can happen."

"Jax, I really need to see you again. I want you in my life forever. You can't just walk in and then leave me like this. What is going to happen? You said you are here without permission?"

"I don't want to be without you either. You just don't know how long I have waited for this."

He then took his hand and started to caress my cheek. He swept his hand ever so softly. Looking at me with the sweetest look a person can ever give you. I felt adored. I felt beautiful. I felt special. No one has ever made me feel like this. I started to caress his other hand. I wanted him to see that I reciprocated the same feelings. I anyone would have walked by and saw us they would have just seen two teenagers being in love.

"Jax, how long have you known about me? How did you know I existed here on earth?"

"It was either by mistake or by fate. I happened to be looking through papers and I found out your information in them. I was about fourteen at the time. Since then I had been planning for this day! I have been dreaming about you for two years now. I loved you before I even knew you."

"Wow Jax, I hear all this and it's so hard to believe that someone can love me this much. This is what soap operas are made of. I just feel that it is all too good to be true and that scares me a lot."

That afternoon we talked so much. I told him all about my life. He told me about his. We laughed and even cried a little. The more I got to know him the more I liked him. At this point I was looking for things that would show me that he was human that he had flaws. I found none. To me he was perfect. He was kind, romantic, handsome, gentle and sweet.

"Do you know that when you came out your door I just froze!" Jax said.

"What! I'm the one who froze!" I laughed

"Your beauty left me without air! I had a whole speech planned out for years and I just took off!" He laughed.

5 THE WAITING GAME

"Kate it's starting to get late. Your parents will worry. Let's stop here. You need time to digest all of this. I promise we will finish this later."

"I guess you are right. I did not even realize how late it was. My parents will be expecting me soon. I don't want to worry them." He was right even though I did not want to stop and leave. But I had to think about my parents, what explanation would I give them? That I was with my friends, would I lie to them? I don't think they could ever believe the truth and they might try to separate me from this boy with crazy stories. No, I needed to get home so I would not stir up any more suspicions. I have been acting so weird and I knew they were already worried enough about their daughter.

Again, he held out his hand and again we walked hand in hand. This must be the way they do things where he is from. The boys here did hold their girlfriends hands but this felt different. I was not complaining. Being held by him even if it was just by a hand felt good. Felt right. His strong hand holding me firmly, telling me you are mine and I am yours.

"Kate, are you all right. Was all this too much for you?" He looked at me with adoring eyes. Oh, how it melted my heart.

"Yeah, I'm ok. Are you? I worry that you will be found and taken away. I need to see you again. What if I never see you, how will we be able to handle it. There is still a lot to say and a lot to sort out."

I seriously feared losing him. I could not let him walk out of my life as swiftly as he walked in. I looked at him and thought to myself "There he is, my heart, my love, my darling Jax"

"I have to admit I worry too but I am taking all the precautions that I need to take. We will meet again.... soon. I can tell you that much. We will figure it out. First I want to finish explaining as much as I can about me, about us. There is so much you need to know. Go home. Live life as normal as you can. We can't have people noticing that there is something wrong with you. For our sake we can't draw any attention to us at this moment. Can you do this?"

"Yes, of course I will. When will I see you again?"

"Soon. As soon as I can."

"Soon, how soon?" My heart needed to know that he would come back for me.

"As soon as I can. I will find you again. Now go my love. Remember you are my heart."

"Bye Jax, I will be waiting. Be safe."

I turned to look at him one last time, our eyes connected and so did our souls.

I made it home. Greeted my parents and ran to my room. I needed to think. So many things were said. Could it be true? Another planet, thousands of them? God. Humans and angels together? Where did Jax come from? What kind of life did he lead? More doubt crept into my heart. Again, how could someone like him (now even more special than before) be in love with me?

I looked at myself in the mirror and studied my reflection. A girl with big brown eyes, long brown hair stared back at me. Average face, average look. I searched and searched to see if I could find what he saw when he looked at me with his intense stares that shook my bones to the core. Nothing. I got nothing. He was this beautiful being and I was just plain Kate.

Days passed and nothing. I went to school and started to act like my normal, peppy self. My friends did not notice anything. My parents were excited for me. My graduation meant so much to them. I ended up going to the prom with some boy that asked me. I knew he always had a crush on me. He was a nice enough boy so I said yes. I dressed up not with any excitement like most of the other girls. It was actually difficult. Like a job. I had to dress up, dance, and pretend to like it.

While at the prom I started to think how different this experience would be if only Jax was at my side. As I danced with my date, I tried to imagine it was Jax. I would be in his arms, he would twirl me around and everything would be perfect. At the end of the night he would even kiss me good night. I looked at my real date and reality stepped in. He was a good date but just as a friend. The night passed, he looked me home a little disappointed I did not want to continue the date at the afterparty everyone was going to but he smiled politely and that was that.

In the same matter I passed my graduation. That was also more for my parents and friends than for myself. I did feel proud of myself and I was happy to see my parents faces as I grabbed my diploma. I was ready for my next stage in life. But what was that stage? College? Jax? Where was he? When would he appear again? Where do I go from here? I had applied to colleges months ago and I was accepted to a few of them, 3 colleges that I really wanted to go to. I just had to pick one.

I needed to talk to Jax soon. I could not take my next step in life without him. I had to decide soon. My parents had been pressuring me to tell them where I was going to go. Plans needed to be made. I understood their point. The three places I could go where so different. I could first of all stay close to home or I could move a little farther from home. Jax, I would move to the moon to be with you. Where are you? Come for me soon.

A few more days passed and I really began to worry. Jax was gone. I had to face it. Gone forever. I cried myself to sleep that night feeling crushed. He said he would be back. Where was he? How could he? He just came into my life and for what? Was it all a joke? If so, how stupid was I to believe in this fantasy! I even believed he was from out of space. How he must be laughing. I was just a dumb teenager. I mean I only saw him literally two times.

How could I feel so much for him? I was so incredibly mad at myself. My first heart break with someone I barely knew. No one knew and no one would ever know. It was like I dated a ghost. If you could even say we dated. It was only two times that we saw each other and the first time we could not even speak to each other that would not constitute as dating. I could not even cry to anyone or vent out my feelings to anyone. Would anyone even believe me?!

All I knew is that I had to pick myself up. Grow up and make a decision to get started on my life. My real life not this fantasy that did not make any sense. This was a tough lesson but maybe I needed it to be able to go into this world and not be a naive little girl. So I took it as a lesson but in reality I was devastated. I woke up from the dream and had to face real life. Life went back to being grey, my smile was forced, and my tears I tasted at night. I quietly sobbed and when I did find my sleep it was Jax's face that I saw every single night. Then I would wake up and realize he was gone and had to experience heart break every morning.

I woke up and told my parents that my choice was made. I would go off to another state to study. I needed a fresh start. I was ready to face my new life. A life without that boy that just came out of the blue to leave without a trace except the hole he left in my heart. I needed to meet new people and explore new places. I was going to study to be a nurse but as I was filling out my college paperwork I decided nursing was not for me. All of a sudden I knew exactly what I was going to study. I was choosing a career that would allow me to travel. I needed to see the world. I would be a journalist. My parents were so surprised at the change but were supportive.

The day came and it was time to go. I was packed up and the tears flooded between my parents and I. They meant everything to me and my new purpose in life was to make them proud. I never mentioned anything that had happened those last days of High School. They hugged me tight and finally I hopped in my new car they bought me as a college present and off I went. I was on my first solo road trip. I looked forward to the alone time while I drove. I wanted to just think and meditate on everything.

As I drove I could not help but to think, what if he comes looking for me and I am gone? What if I made the wrong choice? What if by moving so far he would never be able to find me? What if.... what if... what if.... Then the anger came back. How dare him have this power over me. How dare he just play with my feelings. How dare he. How could he not feel what I felt? Did I just imagine all the feelings, all the heat between us? I kept driving, tears in my eyes. Heart broken. A girl off to start her new life. I felt scared. Would I be able to ever trust again, love again? Only time would tell.

Jax. Jax. Jax. My darling Jax. Even if I had dreamed it all, imagined it all I could not deny the fact that he had become part of me forever. He was there tucked away deep in my soul where I had buried him. I just had to push him in, cover his tracks and put on a smile on my face to confront my new world. My world without Jax.

I arrived at college and it was all a little alarming at first. I found the dorm I would be staying at and met my roommate. She seemed friendly enough. She was already unpacked and went off with her family to show them around. I unpacked and then decided to go for a walk around campus to get familiar with my new home. I wondered what would happen if Jax was to show up at my home asking for me. What would my parents think? I wondered how different this experience of moving to college would be with Jax here with me. How much more exciting it would be. I would be walking around hand in hand with him feeling so proud to be with such a handsome guy.

We could have gotten to know each other in this setting of me being independent. How could he just disappear just as quickly as he appeared in my life? I sat down by a beautiful, huge oak tree that had a little bench next to it. I sat and observed all the people around me. I saw many families walking around together, couples happily chatting away and groups of friends. I was here alone. I had just met my roommate but she was busy with her family so I did not want to tag along and disturb their last moments together.

A boy walked up to me out of nowhere. "Excuse me."

"Yeah?" I asked.

"Are you from here?"

"No."

"Me neither, do you mind if I sit with you for a little bit? I'm feeling kind of out of place. I actually got here yesterday and I am still trying to sit and take it all in for a minute. I can't believe I am really here."

"Yeah, me too."

"By the way, I'm Johnny."

"Nice to meet you Johnny, I'm Kate."

6 THE MEETING (JAX)

I had prepared so long for this moment. It was finally here. What would she do? How will she react? She has no idea. No idea about me or what I mean to her life. She has been a part of my life for what seemed forever and yet she has no clue. My other half, my love, she was my sun, my moon and all of the stars in my sky. I loved her with every cell in my body. One problem. She has no idea I exist and what I am to her and I had to change that.

She opened her front door of her home. I stood there waiting. Waiting for her. My most perfect angel. All of a sudden, the door opened and there she was. What a vision she was. All I could do was stare. She was so beautiful. I was not sure what to do. Was it a good time to go up to her? Should I wait a little longer? Should I wave? Oh no, did I make a mistake?

She looked at me and I stared back. The world stood still. I felt the wind, I smelled the cool breeze and all I could see was her in a long white dress. Something clicked. We clicked. Our eyes were connected and our souls spoke. It was an indescribable language. We spoke with no words. We felt with no physical touch. I could see her eyes questioning who I was. If anyone was to walk by they would see two people standing like statues just gazing at each other. I panicked and all of a sudden I decided that all the words I had practiced vanished. I would not be able to put a sentence together. So, I vanished. I walked off. The moment passed and even though I did not do anything I wanted to all I could think was Wow. So, this is what it was like. I had heard about it all my life. When soulmates come together it was electrifying, indescribable intense feeling of something so great if could not be put into words. It simply was with no explanation of how or why.

As soon as I walked away, the void was back. The empty feeling took over again. Now it was so much worse. I had my soulmate for only a few minutes and for the first time ever I felt what it meant to be connected to someone. Once you feel and experience something that intense you can never go back to being ok with being alone. Loneliness is one of the most devastating feelings a person can have.

I also thought that she must be feeling the same way. I did not want to hurt her in any way. I had so much time to prepare for this but she didn't so I could only imagine how confused she must be feeling. I wished I could be by her side to comfort her like I knew only I could. She was so young. So innocent and I had to be very slow and be able to explain things, things that would not be easy to explain and even harder to comprehend. Even though we were actually just a couple of months apart due to where we came from I was more advanced in wisdom that an earthly boy my age. Avian's where very advanced and had more information available to us than any person on earth.

Our bond was irreplaceable and she had to know why. She had to know that the feelings she felt were so normal. We were meant to be. We were planned to be together since the beginning of time. I had traveled from so far, risked so much and now it was time. I saw her, she saw me and now there was no turning back. Everything was set in motion. My nerves failed me this time but next time it would be different.

I would be seeing her again soon. Hopefully she could believe me. Our fairytale had started and all I had to do was make her believe. Make her believe my incredible story. Not so incredible to me but to her she would need to have to take a leap of faith. Would she be able to handle it? Could she understand it all? I had to risk it and have faith that love could really take on anything. I would soon know the answer to that.

I came from Avian. Avian is a galaxy away from earth. We live differently. Where I am from love is a treasure. Not everyone has it. There we know how it works. We have the knowledge. Knowledge is power. Love was created but not for all. Soulmates where matched in the beginning of time. Only some were lucky enough to meet their soulmates. If you were one of the lucky ones you would be complete. Your cycle would reach its end and then you could ascend higher on your next life.

Your life would consist of living to make that other person happy and the happier you made them the happier you made yourself. Life would be filled with light, colors and music. To be with that person was the closest thing to being in heaven. Finding your other half was not easy. You would have to pick the right path and your other match would have to pick the right choices as well. In order for you to find each other you would both need to be on the right path at the right time.

For those who were not so lucky they lived a different life. They would probably end up marrying a person who did not complete them. They would love and care for them but the type of love could not even come close to the intense passion and love you could receive from your soulmate. They lived their lives always feeling something was missing. They lived never being completely happy, never knowing their other half. Feeling that happiness was almost at their reach but not quite. They would feel sadness in their hearts for they would never be able to know how it felt to experience that kind of love. It is like the love you feel for your mother and the love you feel from a pet. Both are true and exist but you can't compare a mothers love to a love from a pet. Same thing happened with soulmates. It was just on another level.

I was in a unique situation. I learned that my soulmate was not in my planet. I ran into some forbidden papers that were attached to my what humans on earth would call a birth certificate and what we call our arrival papers. I am guessing it was attached by mistake. Everyone has two papers. One tells your specific information and the second your soulmates. They are divided and each individual gets their own. My papers came together and it was then that I learned my soulmate lived on earth.

I quickly realized that this was not fair. How could I be given a fair chance to meet her if she was so far away! I did not know much about this planet earth except that it was a fairly new planet compared to ours. Therefore, humans there would be naive and not understand many things complicating my situation even greater. How could this be? Soulmates where hard to find but never this hard!

I spent the next year studying earth. I wanted to know everything. How they lived, what they did and how much they knew about life. My next obstacle was how I was going to get there and then how I was going to find her. It was hard enough finding your other half in your own planet let alone in one light years away!

I did what I had to do and hid in one of the ships that were off to a mission on earth. It took me months to wait for one to come around and finally here I was on my way to earth to search for my soulmate. After I reached earth with the help of the internet I found out all I needed to know and off I was to meet her. I made it and I saw her. Now it was time to explain to her who I was, who she was, who WE were. I had to succeed after all of this I had to succeed or I would lose it all.

"Hi, I'm Jax" I spitted out.

She was amazing. More than I could ever hope for. How did I get so lucky? If I could have described my perfect girl I could not have gotten it any better. All I wanted to do was grab and kiss her. Hold her and never let her go. Of course, I had to detain myself from doing that. It was soooo hard. I looked at her soft lips and her smooth skin and I just wished I could caress her. I longed to hug her and smell her hair. I could just imagine what it would be like to have her in my arms.

Where to start? What to say? I had to search deep inside me and find the perfect words. I knew one thing. She was worth it. Oh, how she was so worth it.

7 EXPLANATIONS (JAX)

The following meeting was spent me trying to explain to her what I had all my life to prepare and she had only a few days. To be with her was so amazing. We first had a brief conversation in which I did not say too much. I did not want to scare her away. Our feelings were really strong. More than I had imagined they would be. I could see how she was so amazed by these sudden feelings she had as well. Each time I spoke to her I could see how she would look at me wanting to understand more and more. She said so much without saying anything at all. As we sat in that coffee shop the world around us was a blur. I know the waitress came in and out, the food was brought and that we did not eat much. As I started to tell her who I really was and where I was from she seemed to take it in but I could see so many more questions start forming in her head. New questions and of course so understandable.

She was so delicate and vulnerable. If I could just shield her from all the harm that could come to her I would do anything. For now, just getting to this point was a win for me. We walked hand in hand. We were actually walking together. Glaring into each other's eyes. Talking. (Well, I did most of it)

All I could think about was about the touch of her hand. I never wanted to let go. To have her next to me was what I dreamed about for so long. I did not want to let her go....ever. I held out my hand every chance I got. She probably thought it was weird but the truth was that if that was the only touch I could get from her at this point I would take it. What I really wanted was to jump and throw her over my shoulders and run off with her to Avian. I would show her my home and she could learn about my life. Deep inside I knew how this would break so many rules. I never heard about anyone from earth going to Avian to live. It was just unheard of. It simply did not happen. There was an order to things and to life and we had always been taught to respect nature and the way things were.

My Kate. My Katherine. My darling, darling love. If she only knew what she meant to me. I wanted to shower her with all my love. In her earthly culture, I could describe her as my fairytale princess. Except she was no princess she was a queen. My queen. Love. Humans on earth do have it. Except they are unaware that the soulmate theory is real. Sure, they write novels about it, make movies and dream of it but they don't truly know for a fact that it actually does exist. Therefore, they end up marrying the person that comes into their lives by chance or luck. They do not know they should be searching for the one and not settling for just anyone. If they knew the signs they should be looking for they would be more careful in choosing their mate. This explained their high divorce rate.

At the end, I promised her we would meet again. Soon. Little did I know it would not go as I planned. She left and I could not wait to see her again. I missed her already. I turned around and *they* were here. The guardians standing straight and tall were here! Oh no. They had come for me. They found me. My heart sank. Kate. Kate. What would happen now?

"Jax, not good." Jordy, one of our guardians spoke. His voice was deep, strong and stern. "You have committed such a huge mistake. You have to come back home and face your consequences."

"Jordy, I had to. Please, I need more time." I could not believe it would end before it could even start.

"Sorry Jax, but they all know you are here. I can't look the other way. You know the rules."

"Jordy, love is worth everything, I had to risk it all. I had to because she is on Earth and not at home. How else could I have a fair chance?"

"I understand Jax but I don't make the rules. I was sent to fetch you. That's it."

Darn it. Just like that I was back home. Home that did not feel like home. Kate was now my home. How could I fail? I failed her, I failed myself. I could not forgive myself. I was so mad I was shaking. Soon, would not be soon at all.

I stood in the middle on a circle. Surrounded by the elders. The elders ran our galaxy. They were not from our planet or from earth they were from everywhere. No one really knew where they had come from, all we knew is that they worked directly from God and they were the law. They were known for being fair, and just. But how fair and just was the universe with me?

I could not bear to think how Kate would take it. She would think I abandoned her. I would not show up and I can almost see her face of disappointment. I had failed her. I had failed us. I had failed our love. I was supposed to unite us and now....and now I was in such a bad predicament that I did not know what would be of me much less of us. I needed for her to know how much I love her. That if it was up to me I would never, never leave her. I was now light years from her. So far away and I could still smell her sweet perfume, I could still feel her soft hands and see her big brown eyes exploring me, trying to figure me out.

Now I had to explain to the elders why I disobeyed them. I sat here and wondered if they could understand me. They, who did not have mates let alone soulmates. They who did not fall in love or ever marry. Could they understand how strong love is? The power it has. Could they know how it feels to love someone else so much they became your world? I was just a boy. A boy who traveled across the universe to meet a girl. His girl. It was all in their hands now. My life, her life all in the hands of the elders.

8 LIFE GOES ON

......5 Years Later....

"Johnny quick take the shot! That one is going to be awesome."

The article I was writing was on how animals have adapted to living in places they had never had to live in after their homes had been destroyed by people. It would go great with that photograph Johnny just took.

"This will be the perfect one." Johnny exclaimed.

"Yes, we make the best team. You and I will continue to conquer the journalism world."

"You bet." Johnny said then leaned in and kissed me. "We can conquer the world. With you by my side nothing is impossible"

"Time to go home." I was so excited about this new job we had been working on.

My job meant so much. I enjoyed it. I had graduated and quickly accepted a job with a well-known company. Johnny and I had become close these past few years. We realized how well we worked together from the start. He took the most amazing pictures and I wrote the articles. His pictures seemed to complete them. Our boss was so happy to have us. He paired us up and we have been working together ever since. We studied together all through college and became great friends through it all. He understood me. We shared a common passion for our profession. We were lucky that we both were accepted in the same company. We went to school together and now we worked together. I felt in this transition I was not alone like I was when I started college. I had Johnny. After we met that first day we instantly became friends. At first it was because we didn't know anyone and so we looked for each other. Then our friendship grew. We had many classes together so we spent a lot of time getting to know one another. He was such a big support system for me. I could count on him for basically anything I needed and he could count on me.

I could not complain. My life had turned out good. I had left home as a sobbing blubbering teenager. Scared and broken. It took me a long time to pull together. I started college and focused on my studies. All my energy was on passing my classes and learning as much as I could. I was really good at what I was doing. My classes took me from being a kid to becoming a great journalist.

When I graduated one of my professors referred me to the company I now worked for. I went to my first interview and was ecstatic when I found out I got the job. I was even more excited when Johnny applied afterwards and also got in! I was assigned a desk by a window and he had the office next to mine. I was given assignments and I would dive into them. Many gave me the opportunity to travel just as I had wished for. I saw the world and met many new cultures. Johnny and I had many adventures together. How much fun we had on all these work trips.

All I had to do was write about my experiences. This was my dream job. It did not feel like a job at all. All in all I was pretty content with my life. Then Johnny and I started to get closer. We were going on assignments together and it was nice having a companion. He had great talent and I admired him for it. He complemented my work and together we felt we made a great asset to any company.

One day after work he and I were in his dark room developing pictures. He looked at me, leaned over and kissed me. It was a gentle kiss. A soft kiss. Friendly kiss. He was a sweet, charming guy. He was tall, dark and handsome. I kissed him back. I had not realized how lonely I really was. I had not dated much in college. I saw guys here and there but nothing serious. I had put up walls long ago and they were there to this day.

Johnny was very patient. He started to look at me differently. Stealing a kiss from time to time. He would hold me, put his arm around me when we watched TV and he would always be there to open doors, and just do whatever it is that guys usually do for girls. He slowly crept his way into my heart. I cared about him. He was a good guy. I was lucky to have him. He never pushed for too much.

Johnny then moved in and it was official, we became a couple. We never really declared any rules or anything it just became the norm. It felt natural, safe and comfortable. He was warm and loving. He gave me a purpose. We went to work together, came home and made a life at home that to many it would be considered boring but to me it was all that I needed. I was content. I had a companion in him. I knew he would never just leave me because Johnny was safe.

I think he was happy too. He never complained about anything. He was always there. He would cook for me when I was sick and he would go with me to the doctor's office. My parents loved him My friends envied me. The perfect gentleman everyone would comment. He treated me with respect and he was my best friend.

The next logical step was marriage. What was I supposed to say except yes? I would have been crazy to say no to a wonderful man like this. A man that was responsible, paid the bills, fixed up anything needed around the home, treated me like a queen and basically was a man in every sense of the word. He was also good looking and I was attracted to him so our physical, intimate life was also good. No complaints.

Any woman would be jumping for joy for this man. So, why wasn't I? Was I forever broken? Had a few days of my life determined my happiness forever? That was just so stupid to even think about. But there it was in the back of my mind, tucked away in my soul since the day I decided to bury it. Jax. Just thinking of him stirred something up inside of me. Like a burning secret, he would always be.

He was probably somewhere, maybe married, maybe dating. He probably remembered me as the dumb girl he made believe the stupidest things ever. He would be laughing from time to time and telling his stories to his buddies. How stupid was I? How could I still even thing about him? He did not deserve one thought coming out of me.

Then it would all come rushing back to me. I closed my eyes and saw his face. His blue eyes again looking at me. How could he fake that? Him holding out his hand for me and taking my hand it so gently into his. Him talking to me and looking at me with so much love in his words. I felt the love. How could it be fake? When he called me "my darling" his voice was so gentle and so full of love. Just a few hours with him had filled me up with a lifetime of longing. Of wishing. Of trying to forget. Not even sweet Johnny could erase his memory.

It was not fair. It was not fair to me and not fair to Johnny. Johnny who had always stood by his word. He did not lie to me. He told me he loved me and stuck around. He was real. He was dependable. I could trust him. He gave me everything. I wish I could feel for him what I felt for Jax. I did love him in my own way but this love did not compare to the love I felt for Jax. Maybe if I would have met him first or if Jax never appeared into my life things would be different between us. Maybe Johnny would have been my one true love.

When Johnny would kiss me it was tender and loving. It was nice. It was very romantic. I never got to kiss Jax but I could only imagine it would be explosive, passionate, the kind of kiss that could start a fire. But then again what did I know. It could just be my imagination. It was not fair to Johnny to compare him like that. He could not compete with a stranger he did not know about and he shouldn't have to. He had earned his way to my life. He did not have to compete with a ghost. I was mad at myself to even be thinking about these things.

Pretty soon I would be Mrs. Johnny Walker. I imagined us living a good life. We would go on our assignments. Do amazing work together. Eventually even start a family. What was wrong with that? A typical life I would say. A life that anyone would envy. I had to face my reality, be grateful and live the life I was given. I had to appreciate all of my blessings. Leave the childish fantasies in the past and grow up once in for all. That was my true destiny. I had to stop these silly fantasies of this silly boy coming back to me. That simply was not going to happen. This was real life and that was just a dream. A dream that ended a long time ago, in another lifetime really.

I always thought that love was not the biggest thing in my life and would never be ever since I got over Jax's heartbreak. I mean why fall in love like that again? That would just be risking getting your heart trampled on again. I was fine with the love that Johnny offered. It was a stable, dependable type of love because that was just how he was. That would be more than enough for me. I could be happy with this. I could definitely live a happy, peaceful life. I would be working doing something I loved, traveling and it would be good. Sometimes when I went for my runs in the park I would see couples kissing and being cuddly together. I wondered if they knew all of that could just lead to great suffering. I was glad I was not risking my emotions in that way anymore. I had control this time. I was a mature woman and this was a mature love. Johnny was the perfect man for someone like me. The best part was is that he seemed to be ok with our life as well. He did not expect all this passion or this public displays of kissing and stuff. I think he understood that this was the way adults love each other, after all this was not a love novel. My mind was made up, this was they life I was going to live and I would marry him. We could definitely have a really good life together. Why not?

9 WEDDING BELLS

Here I was all dressed in white. The day had come, my wedding day. It was supposed to be the day that all little girls dream about. It was supposed to be a turning point in my life. A day I would remember and treasure forever. My hair and makeup was done. Something old, something borrowed, something blue...done. Friends and family waited outside. My parents gleamed. They arrived last week to help with all the last minute details. A limo awaited for me outside ready to take me to church.

"Mom, can you give me a minute. I just need to be alone for a little bit. "

"Sure, sweetie. I'll be outside when you are ready. I know your nerves must be taking over, just remember it's all the excitement!" My mom smiled and went outside happily. I wondered who was happier, probably she was. This was as much her day as it was my day. I was glad to be giving it to her.

She closed the door and I kept staring at myself in the mirror. Who was I? This was my day. Was this right? Most of all I asked myself where was my excitement at? I thought I should be feeling the feelings I got when I was with Jax, but I wasn't. Even the first day I saw him I felt more joy than what I felt today. Why? I kept trying to convince myself how lucky I was and how happy I should be feeling. I shouldn't have to be convincing myself though. I should just be happy, period.

I wondered if this was a mistake. Would I regret this decision later? Johnny sure did not deserve this. He deserved a girl who did get excited to see him. I did not want to hurt him in any way. He was waiting for me at this moment feeling so happy, just like I should be. I never told him or anyone about Jax. I held on to that piece of my life for myself.

Jax. Jax. Jax. Where are you Jax? I closed my eyes and I called to him. My soul called to him. My heart implored for him to appear. Like if he would magically show up. I wanted to believe in him. I wanted him to be true. Jax, please I need you, I need you to come NOW. It is now or never. PLEASE JAX COME FOR ME. STOP ME. I believe. Where are you? If you were true and not a figment of my imagination, come to me, my love. I forgive you but please come. It has to be right now.

What happened to all this thinking about mature love and being sensible? All those thoughts disappeared and all of a sudden my heart seemed to want to burst out and have a say so. I wanted to scream and yell and cry for Jax. Like a spoiled little child when she wants her mommy. I wanted Jax with every part of me. I needed him so bad it physically hurt.

I broke down. I did not want to act like this but I had to admit I wanted him to be here. I wanted him to come and I would forget everything. I would run away with him anywhere even to another universe. I was now a grown up and I could easily go. I would be willing to leave everything for him. Jax, you are my soulmate. Come. I felt a little childish standing here imploring for a miracle to happen. I could not stop the tears. I did not care about my makeup. I cried just like all those years ago. I opened up the wound again and it felt just as raw as it did a long time ago.

Jax, you came once out of nowhere. Come again. I sat on my bed and nothing. I heard people talking outside my door, birds singing outside my window but no Jax. No blonde hair, blue eyed boy was anywhere. No one was holding their hand to take my hand. How my heart hurt. Somewhere he existed. Somewhere he was living his life. His life without me. Could he be with someone else? Could someone else be receiving his love? Could his gentle touch be going to another lucky girl? No. No. No. I couldn't bear the thought. I would trade myself for that other girl if I could. I knew I was being desperate, dramatic even. There was nothing I could do.

No, Kate. I told myself. Pull yourself together, dry those tears. Put your big girl panties on and face your life. You are a grown woman living a wonderful life. You have your love waiting for you out there. Do not lose him. Do not do this to him. Your family is out there. Your friends are out there. You have a career. You travel the world. You have everything. Do not be stupid and throw it out for something that at this point you probably imagined. It was probably all a dream. A childish dream.

In that instance,, I realized Jax was not coming. Jax was gone...forever.... for good. I had to grow up forever too. Mature for good. No going back from here on out. I had to say good bye to Jax once and for all. Jax, I loved you without you deserving my love. I loved you without understanding this love. I loved you without even having kissed you! I loved you. Now I have to let you go. I am freeing this love and I understand you were just a dream. I have woken up and now I need to live my life. Bye my darling blonde, blue eyed boy. Bye. This day, my wedding day I broke up with Jax.

"Mom, Mom." I called out to my mother trying to make my voice sound happy. "I am ready. Get dad let's go"

My mother came in and saw me with all my mascara running down my face.

"Kate, are those tears of happiness?"

"Yes, mom, I am ready to get married. Will you touch up my makeup." I tried to give her a smile.

She quickly redid my makeup and hugged me.

"Kate, I hope you are very happy. You are the prettiest bride I have ever seen in my life. My little girl is going to start her new life."

"Yes, mom I am."

I made it to the doors of the church. With my dad at my arm I had to face my reality. With every step I took I did not know if I was walking towards my happiness or my doom. I looked up and saw Johnny standing at the end with a radiant smile and teary eyes. My heart felt something. He was such a good guy. I knew I could not hurt him. I had to believe that this was love. What I felt for Jax was something else. It was obsession, infatuation or I don't know lust or passion? I had to stop comparing them.

When it was time to say my vows. I stopped. I looked around the church. I knew that I was searching for HIM. This was it. Those blue eyes where were they? Jax, this is it. Ok, no Jax. I felt betrayed again even though he did not know I was getting married. I could not be mad at him for this. But I was, because he was supposed to be the one. He was supposed to come back like he promised. He was never supposed to let me go and here I was marrying another man. It was supposed to be him.

I turned faced Johnny and vowed to be with him in sickness and in health. I would do everything in my power to be a good wife to him. I would love him. I would respect him. I looked at him and hugged him tight. He was now my husband. He was my love. And that was that. No turning back now. Our promises were made to each other in front of God and in front of everyone.

The rest of the day went by fast. The reception came, we danced, we laughed and we held each other. At the end of it we quietly escaped and drove off to start our new life as husband and wife. It would not be our first time sleeping together but it was different now. We were now married. Like always it was sweet, it was nice. And just like that life moved on.

......JAX.....

"Jax. Jax. Come Jax. Please I need you."

I heard her. Kate. Kate needs me. My heart pounded, she needed me, she wanted me. I wanted to take off. Risk it all again. Was she ok? Something was happening. I felt something deep inside of me. I felt like a chunk of me was ripped out and I was so scared I would lose her forever. I couldn't, I couldn't wait any longer.

The elders had made a pact with me. That day that I was caught had changed everything but I was given another chance. This time it would have to be how they planned it. I was given a sanction. For my disobedience and trying to take matters into my own hands instead of trusting fate or letting nature decide I had to wait 5 years to make a trip to earth again. 5 long years. Then they would allow me to come back to search for Kate.

Things in my world ran according to rules. Everything had its place, everything was orderly and this is why our world lasted for so long. We had no wars, no violence and lived peacefully with each other. They told me after these 5 years I would be going to earth to work as a "advisor". I would be of age then and would be given a mission to work helping humans. They needed as much help as possible. I would then travel legally and during my time there I could search for Kate.

I had no choice but to accept. I made it home that day feeling destroyed. I wished there was some way to let Kate know what was happening. I could not bear to think the hurt I caused her. What she must be thinking. I let her down. She must hate me. I hated me. My heart ached. There was no-one to blame but myself. I was so angry. I should have waited and done things right. Now it was done. All I could do was count the days to meet her again.

Today 5 years later I felt her. I felt her calling. Something inside of me shifted. I needed to go. She needed me. This was the universe telling me I had to do something. I ran to the elders and asked them if it was time. After all five years had passed. They all looked at each other and nodded.

"Yes, it's time. Get your stuff you are leaving" They replied.

10 UNEXPECTED SURPRISES

"Honey, honey wake up we are late" Johnny exclaimed. "It's eight o'clock already!"

"What! Let's go!"

I jumped out of bed, ran to the bathroom and started to get ready. We had been staying at a hotel in Atlanta for our current assignment. Our plane was scheduled for 11 o'clock today to go back home. We had gone out last night something that is totally out of the norm for us. We are usually homebodies dedicating almost all our time to our work. You would see me typing away at my laptop and Johnny working on his photographs. Last night we tried to go out like a "normal" couple. We had dinner and then went to a club to see what experience we could have. We quickly discovered it is not our lifestyle. The music was way too loud. The crowd was mostly drunk and cigarette smoke was everywhere. This was not fun for us.

We grabbed our clothes, stuffed them in our luggage and ran out to take our plane. Our baggage was checked in and we were now sitting in our assigned seats on the plane.

"We made it." I turned to Johnny and smiled.

"Yes, but I almost thought you would choke when you wolfed down your Danish this morning! You were not leaving without breakfast huh! "Johnny laughed.

I giggled. He was always in good spirits. Always with a smile making the best out of any situation. What would I do without him? Probably miss a plane! I laughed and leaned my head on him. Johnny, so reliable, so safe, he always knew how to lift my spirits. He was the best companion ever.

Life with him was good. We had our routine. We both loved our jobs and if it wasn't for the fact that we worked together we would have much time to be together at all. We could dive into our work and easily be consummated by it all day. Sometimes forgetting to even stop to eat. It wasn't that we needed the money so bad or that we had to, it was just that we enjoyed it that much. We were fortunate that our hobby was our job. We got paid for what we loved to do and we were so lucky that we got to do it together.

I woke up the next day and I saw Johnny was out of bed. I brushed my teeth and went down to the kitchen. My eyes widened at what I saw. There was Johnny with the cutest thing on earth. He had this furry thing in his arms with a big red bow on it. Oh, my goodness, I ran and took it. It was a puppy. He bought me a puppy! I loved it.

"I figured it was time to widen our family! I know that we travel but I already spoke to Bill at work and he will take the dog in anytime we need him to."

"Great because that was my only concern, a babysitter, or in this case a dog-sitter!"

"What can we name him?" Johnny asked.

"Jax!"

What! Did I just say Jax? It came out without me even thinking about it! How could I just spurt that out like that? I never spoke to Johnny about him or to anyone else for that matter.

"I mean, I mean or we can name him Baxter or any other name" I tried to take it back.

"No, Jax it is." Johnny stated. "I like Jax, Where did you ever come up with that name hun?"

"Ummm, I don't know it just came to me I guess" I blushed feeling guilty.

So Jax it was. My dog, Jax. He immediately took to me. He followed me around everywhere and I fell in love with my new fur baby. Jax. Every time I called to him my heart would skip a beat. Why did I name him Jax? Another Jax in my live that came to it unexpectedly. This Jax would not leave me. He loved me with the purest of love. Oh Jax, I hugged him tight. How I wish.... how I wish .... No, no Kate do not do this to yourself. How can I wish for Jax again? Don't put yourself through this. I can't live life like this, wondering, what if... No. Stop. Jax is your doggy. That's it. Do not relate one with the other. Who was I kidding? I did relate this dog, this innocent dog with my Jax. I pretended that by hugging him I was hugging Jax. It was even nice to be able to say his name out loud for everyone to hear. Jax, Jax, Jax. By having him near I had Jax nearby. Johnny saw how much I loved this dog and it made him happy. If he only knew! Again the guilt took over me. The guilt, the pain and the silent tears.

Jax, was quickly growing although not too much because he was just a shih tzu so he did not grow too big. He turned into my shadow so much that there was no babysitter for him. He ended up going to all our trips with us. I could not bear to be without my Jax. I could not leave him. I did not want this Jax to leave my life and I would not permit it from happening this time.

Johnny was given an assignment to go to New York. I was not going this time because I was going to the doctor to do some lab work. I had not been feeling so good lately. This was very unusual for us since we were always together. I told Johnny I was going to go ahead and take Jax to the vet as well. He did not mind me staying behind. Like always doing everything to make me happy. He did not complain when I brought Jax everywhere. He could not even imagine how much I grew to love this dog but he accepted it and teased me about it saying how this was my new baby, that we now had a son!

The morning he left, I woke up and felt something different in the air. It was just a weird feeling inside of me. I could not pin point exactly why I as feeling this way. I did know I wasn't feeling my best. I got dressed and opened the door to our backyard to let Jax out and to go get some fresh air. Maybe that would make me feel better.

I froze. He was there! Jax. Not the dog.

Jax. The boy. The blonde, blue eyed boy.

Again.

I was reliving my past.

Why after all these years was he here?

How did he find me?

What to do?

What to say?

All I could do was stand there frozen just like the first time.

It seems I have always been like this frozen in time.

Time stood still.

My soul froze.

So many questions.

How could it be?

How did the world return him to me?

Is he a dream?

Is it real?

Am I?

11 REVELATIONS

No, this was not happening to me again. I walked up to him and stood there. We literally could not take our eyes off each other. All of a sudden he grabbed me and kissed me. Just like that. It was a kiss full of passion, full of anger and at the same time full of love. Pure love. Our first and only kiss. I had never felt this before. I felt every pore of my body completely submitted to him. I knew again I was sucked in. I was his. Completely his.

How did he have this power over me? Feeling his lips on my lips was heaven, pure heaven. I felt his arms around me and I had my hands around him. It took a while for us to stop. I was so afraid. I did not want to stop but I knew that if I didn't I would not be able to have any control of anything else that could happen between us. Jax. My Jax. His smell, his touch, and now his lips.

Tears started flooding out of me. I turned to a complete idiot. I was so angry. I was thinking how could he come back and at the same time what took him so long! All the feelings of anger disappeared and quickly got mixed with feelings of love and fear, fear of him leaving. I was rattled. He confused me.

"Jax. Why?" That is all I could manage to get out.

"My love, my darling. I'm back."

Jax dried my tears with his hands and then took my hand and we walked over to an outdoor patio set and we sat down. "I have much to say to you. I can explain everything. I never really got a chance to finish explaining the first time but now I will"

"Jax I don't know if I can go through this again. Besides I am not the same girl. A lot has happened. You left me and never came back!"

How could he possibly have an explanation? How could he possibly make it up to me? How could I forgive him? Deep inside I knew I already did. He was actually here. In front of me. He was sitting there looking as handsome as always. My Jax, in my own backyard. Oh, how I wish things were different. How I wanted to just grab him, be in his arms, kiss him and do so much more.

All of a sudden Jax, the dog came running to him and jumped on him like he knew him. Both Jax's where playing like they belonged together. I sat there dumbfounded just looking at them like if this was the most normal scene! How I wish it was OUR dog, and this was OUR life together. How beautiful it would be. How just by thinking about it the world around me had changed. Everything became brighter. Hope existed, possibilities opened up, the world became a different world, a world full of endless possibilities. Sounded cheesy, I know but love does that to you.

But it wasn't. I was married. Johnny was real. Jax had left. Reality settled in. No, this was not real. This is just another dream that would end and then what. Then I would be left again crushed, wondering what had just happened. I did not deserve this. I don't think I could bear it. I had to stop this right now before it was too late.

"Jax, stop!" Both the dog and the boy froze and looked at me.

"Kate, is this a bad time? There is a lot we need to discuss and this time I don't want no interruptions."

"Actually, this is not the best place for you to be at." I had to set boundaries out of respect for Johnny. My husband. He deserved that much.

"Just tell me when and where, this time around you set the terms."

I thought for a minute and knew that what he deserved and what I should do is tell him never. I should have told him that I was married, he left me and life went on. He needed to know things had changed. I grew up. I had a life now. He could not just walk in and walk out as he pleased. That was not acceptable. I would not put up with it. I had to be firm. The next thing I know the words that came out of my mouth did not match those in my head.

"How about tomorrow 9am sharp? Do you know the running trail on Park Way?"

"I will find it."

"Will you really?" I needed to know he would be there.

"I will be there and finally we will clear things up. "

He got up to leave. He was looking at me. I got up and faced him. We stood there facing each other not really sure what to do or what was going to happen. I could feel the electricity between us. It could probably light up a whole city. I felt so drawn to him. He was like a magnet to me. In his eyes I could get lost in. They were such a deep blue color. His sweet, sweet mouth. He was so gorgeous. His strong arms that held me tightly just a few minutes ago. It was now too late. My heart was his again. My heart was yelling for him to grab me again. Kiss me. Hold me. Don't go. Don't leave me, ever. He started to walk away. No! Don't! Come back. Please come back. I wanted to scream.

"Jax!" OMG I actually called him. I meant to say it in my head but it came out loud and clear.

He turned around looking straight at me.

"Jax." I ran to him. I took his hand in mine. "Please, don't go. I need you."

"I need you too. So much."

"Jax." I started to cry.

"No, my love don't cry. I'm so sorry." He grabbed me and hugged me.

Again, I was in his arms, where I knew I belonged. I felt so good to be there. We fit. Everything was good.

"Jax." I whispered "I love you so much."

"I love you more than you can imagine. Kate, what I wouldn't do for you. You have no idea how much I have already done."

I wondered what he meant. I wondered if he had any idea what I went through. If he could only understand how much I really loved him. I wondered what he would say if I told him he meant everything to me. How he would react if he knew. If he only knew I was his. I was his in every way that truly means to belong to someone.

He grabbed my face and again another kiss.

You can kiss a thousand guys in your life but if you are not kissing the right person you have not really kissed anyone at all. Kissing him was like kissing for the first time. Life around me disappeared. Nothing existed. It was just Jax and me. I felt his hand on my back placed there pressing me towards his chest. Then he let me go gently. I felt like I was going to faint.

"I will see you tomorrow my darling."

And just like that he was gone.

I stood there for what seemed forever. Lost in my thoughts, unable to digest what had just happened. He took my breath away and at the same time filled me up with life. I woke up. I had been in trance and I was awake....again. Jax had this power over me. Just like that I believed him and just like that all that love rushing came back. It had been asleep and now it was wide awake. It did not matter what made or what did not make sense anymore. I considered myself to be an intelligent woman yet when it came to Jax I would turn to a complete idiot.

Wow, but he was back. He was actually here and we kissed. I dreamed for this day to come so many, many times but I never thought it would actually come true. I had practiced all the ways I would tell him off and send him on his way. I also practiced all the ways I would throw myself in his arms and he would carry me off into the sunset. Just like it happened in the story books that I use to read when I was young. This was real life though. I was supposed to scream and yell at him and tell him to leave and never come back. Yeah, that did not happen.

I was going to see him again. Oh, my gosh, I was going to see my boy again! I could not contain my excitement. Loving this boy was as natural for my body as sleeping was. He lit a spark in me like nothing or no one could. It was kind of scary how his smile could make me just forget everything. I don't think I would be sleeping much tonight because my blonde, blue eyed boy was back and now my world had been rocked.

I was so lucky that Johnny was out of town. Of all the times he could have shown up he appeared when Johnny was not here. Was that pure luck or just fate? I felt bad doing this behind Johnny's absence. This was not in my nature. I had never cheated on him before. I had to think though, with Jax it was now or never. I needed to hear him out to see what possible explanation he had for disappearing on me. It was the only way that I could close this chapter in my life. Maybe this was the way to get over him.

After this last meeting, I could finally feel free. Yes, I convinced myself, this is something I had to do. I had to do this for me and also for Johnny's sake. The kiss, that was just unexpected. Wow, that kiss came without words, without warning. That kiss was a kiss. I could still taste his lips on my lips. I think I was in trouble.

12 HEAVEN

That night just as I thought I hardly slept. I could not wait for the next day to come. What would happen? What could he possibly tell me? I felt so woozy just like I did all those years back. I was a giddy school girl once again. I felt the butterflies. I had goosebumps all over just thinking about our meeting. He was here again, here in my heart and most of all present in my life. I felt him with every heartbeat. He lived in me. He was a part of every breath I took. How could I feel such a great love when he didn't deserve it? It was so illogical. Crazy even.

I woke up in the morning and just could not believe I would see him again today, just a few hours from now. My blonde eyed boy. He was in my town. He had kissed me. I still tasted him. His sweet, sweet kisses. I felt like running to him. Just like this in pajamas and all. How crazy is that! I just wanted to run into his arms and grab him, kiss him and never let him go again. What was I going to do? How could I hold myself back and control my emotions?

I ate some cereal for breakfast because it was all I could keep down. My nerves were at an all-time high. I ran upstairs to get ready. What to wear? I had to look perfect. Oh, my God, I felt like a school girl getting ready for a date with her high school boyfriend. There I was feeling so excited like I did not feel with Johnny.

I felt such happiness. I never was the person who cared that much how I looked. I was a simple girl. Usually I would throw on some jeans and a t-shirt, pulled my hair back in a ponytail, smacked on some lip-gloss and I was good to go. Now today I cared about every detail even how my socks looked. I decided on some skinny jeans and a pretty blouse I had bought recently. I let my hair loose, put on a little of my lip-gloss and some perfume and I thought I looked ok.

As I went to grab my keys to head out I looked at my hands and they were actually shaking. I hopped in my car and sped off. I would be there in time. As I pulled into the parking lot I spotted him. He took my breath away. Even from afar he held such a strong hold over me. Jax, what will you tell me? Will today change my life like it did before? I was scared. Scared what would happened if he stayed in my life and scared of what would happen if he didn't.

"Hi." I said as I reached him.

All of a sudden, he grabbed me and held on to me really tight. "Thank you for coming." His eyes twinkled and he gave me that radiant smile of his.

"I'm here, now I need to know. I need to know everything this time. Please help me to understand why you left me? Help me to understand why you lied and made me look like a fool and then just left. I actually believed that you were from another planet! Stupid right! I was a schoolgirl, easy target for you huh?"

I felt angry just saying those words to him but more than angry I felt hurt, wounded, confused and anxious.

"Ok, finally you will know everything. I wanted to tell you so much and did not get a chance to. Today you will know."

"First you need to know I did not lie to you. I am from another place. I tell you the truth when I say I am from another universe. I am not from earth. This is the hardest part but I know that you do believe me. You knew it then and you know it now. Hold my hand I can actually show you a peek of where I am from. Since we are connected I can transfer some of my memories to you but you have to believe."

Jax took my hand and closed his eyes. I closed my eyes as well because I wanted to believe.

Then I started to see images. It was a planet. It was very similar to ours but at the same time so different. I saw Jax there. He was with a group of people. They were all older men and he was in the middle of them. Then he was somewhere else. It was like a glass house. Everything is clean, modern looking and beautiful. Jax was at a table looking at a piece of some crystal, must be some jewelry of some sort. Then everything went blank.

Jax, let my hand go.

"Sorry I can only do this for so long."

"I saw you!, I saw!" Was he telling the truth?

"Yes, that is just a glimpse of my home. Remember I told you I was not supposed to be here on earth looking for you that I could be taken back? Well, I was. After I dropped you off I was caught."

As he continued to tell me the rest. I realized the mistake I had made. He had told me he was running a risk. I just assumed he left and he didn't leave me! He never left me. He loved me too!

"Oh, Jax. I am soooo sorry. I just thought you left. I could never have imagined what you went through. You risked everything for me. You found me... twice. Across the universe you found me."

We kissed. Like always it was right. It was heavenly. I was in heaven here with him I had found paradise. He was my soulmate, my love, my darling. We were literally a match made in heaven. My Jax, my boy.

"I love you so much." I told him "I never stopped, even as angry as I was with you, I never stopped. I wanted to. I told myself I hated you. I told myself that it was all a joke or a bad dream but I never stopped loving you at all. "

"Kate, now we can be together for ever. We can live out our fate. We have always been destined to be together. Nothing can tear us apart. It is the right time for us."

Tears rolled out of my eyes. How could I tell him? I was married now. Johnny existed. He did not deserve me leaving him. I would break his whole world just like once he broke my whole world. I would disappoint Jax. Here I was married to the best man (the best earthly man) and he adored me but would I have to tear down his whole world to pieces? How could I tell Jax this?

"What is wrong?"

"Jax, there is something I have to tell you now. Something I must explain to you"

"Tell me, there is nothing you can't say to me Kate. I want to know everything and anything about you. I will always be here not matter what. Why are you so upset?"

"Jax, I'm married."

13 BROKEN DREAMS (JAX)

I had planned our encounter to be a certain way. I wanted to plan it and for it to be special. I wanted to study her a bit before approaching her. But I was standing in her backyard trying to decide what the next move was. All of a sudden, the backdoor opened up and there she was. Just like that she was standing not across the universe but a few feet away from me. I could swear to you the sky changed, the clouds changed even the grass under my feet changed.

The world around me came alive. She looked a little different. More grown up. More beautiful than I had remembered her. This time everything was different. No time to waste. I went up to her kissed her, grabbed her, pulled her to me and I kissed her with all the passion that a man can use on a woman. Oh, how I had missed having her near. The kiss was incredible. She was incredible. I never wanted to let her go.

Kate, my beautiful other half was mine. Now I was here with permission from the universe. It was right. It was our time. I had a lot of explaining to do. This time she would hear me out. She would understand. We weren't kids this time around. I was a man and she was a woman. A man and a woman that were going to be together as one. My girl. My darling. My Kate.

After we decided to meet the next day. I was there two hours early! I sat down and was practicing what I would say to her. I needed for her to know that I did not leave her. Most of all that I would never, ever leave her again. We were together now and no force of nature could tear us apart. We could have our life together. We could be so happy. A lifetime with her would not even be enough for me but luckily, I knew we would be together forever because that's what soulmates do once they find each other. They are together forever.

She came up from behind me and I turned around. Looking at her and feeling like my life was about to change. We could finally start building our life together. Then she said those words that broke my heart. My world came tumbling down. My plans were crushed.

"Jax, I'm married. "

I had to sit down. I looked down and was speechless. This I had not planned for. How could I have not imagined this! A wonderful, amazing, girl like Kate. Of course, she would have found someone. The possibility never crossed my mind. Any guy would be crazy not to want to be with her and fight to win her over. Someone actually did and was blessed to have her as a wife.

All of a sudden I felt what I never felt before. I felt like I had been punched in the gut. I felt rage and jealousy. I was so jealous of this unknown guy I had no clue about. Who had the greatest pleasure of being able to have united their life to hers? Who was so fortunate to having had a "yes" from *my* Kate. Who? Who was this guy that I would forever hate. Who beat me to her?

"Jax, I'm so sorry. I didn't know. I just knew you left. I waited for you for years. I even called out to you on my wedding day! I begged the universe to bring you to me. I cried and cried out your name. My soul was calling out to you. All I received was silence!"

Kate fell to her feet sobbing.

"No, Kate, in no way was it your fault. How could I expect you to do anything else but continue to live your life? You didn't know. I was yanked out of your life and all you had was the memory of this strange boy that walked in and out of your life in a minute. In no way it is your fault"

I could not help but to have a few tears fall from my eyes as well. I grabbed my love and lifter her up. We hugged. No words just two heartbroken souls together feeling mutual grief and not knowing how the universe could be so cruel.

"I actually felt you calling out to me! I felt you calling me. I knew it was you. Kate, I'm sorry I was not able to get here sooner. I'm so sorry"

"No, it's not your fault either. I guess it is our destiny. Maybe that is why we were born in different planets. Maybe we weren't meant to be. Maybe we are one of the ones that weren't supposed to meet in this lifetime."

"Noooo, no Kate. No."

I did not expect this bomb. What could I do with this new information?

She was married. Married! She belonged to someone else. No, I could not accept this. Fate was playing a trick on us. This was not fair. I had done things correctly this time, I had played by the rules. Why?

"Kate, do you love him?"

I had to ask even though I was not sure I could take her answer.

"Yes. He is a good man. He loves me and is good to me but..."

She loves him. No, how could she?

"...it is not like I love you. With him it is different. It is simple love. A caring type of love. He is nice and he is like my best friend. I don't want to hurt him. He is a wonderful person."

"That love can't compare to what I feel for you Jax. You actually take my breath away. I feel you in every pore of my body. I see you and it physically hurts just to see you walk away. You are here and just knowing we have to part in a little while makes me miss you already and you are not even gone yet. With you there is passion, love and it is so hard to explain. You are my true love. His love can't compare. I do love him but he is not you Jax. "

"Kate, oh Kate, I came back too late"

"Jax, what do I do?"

Again we hugged tight.

"I can't let you go."

"Don't"

I kissed her in the cheek. I kissed her in her forehead. Then I kissed her in her lips. I needed her. I kissed her like it was the end of the world. I caressed her arm, her back and the back of her neck. I needed her. We kissed for what seemed forever. Each of us not wanting to stop. We felt if we stopped then it would mean the end for us. I did not want that to happen. Kate was my forever.

"I can't live without you! Jax, I have this life that I never really felt part of. I need you. I can't be without you."

"Kate, I can't ask you to do what I want you to do. What I want you to do is selfish. I want you to love me. I want you to pick me, no pick us. We deserve our love to grow and take us to places we know nothing about. Places only you and I can go together. You are a part of me as I am a part of you. I want to hold you and take you away. I know though that it's totally your choice to make. I'm sorry to put this on you. Take some time. Think about what you want to do and I will understand and respect whatever you decide. No matter what I will always be here for you. I need some time to digest all of this too."

So that was that. We agreed to think things over. As I walked away. The world went gray. The sun did not shine as bright. My life was changed. I was so happy this morning and now I walked back to my apartment completely disillusioned. All I could do was wait. More waiting. It seems that all my life would consist of a waiting game. I had a lot to think over. Kate had even more to think over. I was devastated but now it was all in her hands.

14 DECISIONS

My head started to hurt with all these thoughts twisting and twisting in my brain. I had to break someone's heart. It would either be Johnny's, or Jax's or my own because by breaking anyone's heart I would also be breaking my own heart. I could not bear to think about either scenario. The next day I had my lab work done and I took Jax to the vet. I tried to stay as busy as possible. I wanted my mind to be occupied but it was impossible. Everywhere I looked I was reminded of my situation. I even started to see shadows around me. I would jump up thinking it might be Jax but when I looked up I saw no one. I was expecting to see his big blue eyes. Expecting is probably not the right word, hoping is more like it.

Why me? Why me? I was not anyone special. Any other girl would give her right arm to be in my shoes. Not me. I had to pick between my husband who I swore to love till death do us part. My sweet husband, who has never, ever said or done anything bad to me. Instead has been a wonderful partner. He was also my best friend. We shared our love for our jobs and were better at them because of each other. We had a home, a dog, a life together. We shared memories, a past, history. Our families were involved. We had traveled the world together. Always having a wonderful time, making amazing memories everywhere we went.

On the other hand, I had Jax. The boy of my dreams. The one who completed me. He made my heart beat faster. He who with just a few stolen moments stole my heart. He was made for me and I for him. Even though he had not been in my life for pretty much all of it, at least not physically. He had been in every dream, every aspiration, every smile, every tear. He had been so present in my mind that it did feel that he had always been with me. Deep inside of me, he never left.

Another day passed and I realized I did not have a way to contact Jax and Johnny was due home in two days. What was I going to do? What if Johnny found out about Jax? What if he didn't? How could I explain this? Jax had walked into my life again and again turned it upside down.

I stared out my window looking at the moon and the stars hoping to find an answer. As I gazed at our amazing sky and thought how beautiful life was I realized that the beauty I saw was not the stars and the moon. The beauty I was seeing was the way I was feeling because Jax was back into my life. I looked up at the moon and wondered if Jax was looking at it too. What he must be going through. It had to be hard for him to hear this. If it was the other way around I don't know how I would have taken the news.

He came back and suddenly everything was different. My world was beautiful. Just the thought of being able to have him in it made my life incredible. I felt the luckiest girl in the universe to have been matched up with him. My boy. I knew what I had to do. I think I always knew. He was my world. Without him my world was dim. I wanted to run to Jax and tell him. I had no clue how to do that. I guess now I was the one that had to wait.

I woke up the next morning with a phone call. It was the doctor. He wanted to tell me the results of my tests. Ina just a few minutes my world crumbled. Now it would be me that would disappear from Jax's world. How could this be? The timing was just so bad. Was this the universe answering my dilemma for me?

I went to the back yard and sat to wait to see if Jax would come by. I had to talk to him. I needed to explain. I needed to understand all of this myself. Jax, Jax where are you? I decided to go to the park where we had met. There he was. Sitting looking out at a pond with ducks. He looked like an angel in my eyes. He was sad.

I thought to myself, there goes my life. There goes my boy, my Jax. There goes my world. There is the boy that was made for me. The only boy in this and every universe that could possibly exist. He was everything to me and now I had to deliver the news.

I took a deep breath and walked towards him.

I tapped him on his shoulder. He turned around a big smile formed but quickly melted away when he saw the look on my face. He looked down and tears started to come down his cheeks.

"Jax, I'm sorry." I cried.

"I understand." He mumbled.

"No, you don't. I'm pregnant." I yelled out. "I just found out! I was going to tell you that I pick you. That you are and have always been the boy of my dreams, the boy of my life. I was so happy and so determined. I was going to give everything up and run away with you. Then I received a call. The doctor says I am about 6 weeks along."

The look on his face I will never forget. I just broke him like he once broke me. I destroyed all our dreams with that sentence. He touched my stomach and closed his eyes. I felt a sort of warmth feeling all of a sudden.

He looked up at me and said, "I just blessed your child. He will be a wonderful son."

"Son?"

"You will have a boy. He is a part of you and I know he will bring you so much happiness. You made the right choice."

"Jax, it's not fair. I was going to pick you. It was always you."

"I know."

"This just changes everything. This baby is innocent. Johnny is innocent too. I just can't do this. The guilt would kill me"

Jax put took my face with his hands and pushed a hair on my face back ever so gently. He stared into my eyes with the deepest, saddest look I had ever seen. His baby blues sparkled with wet tears.

"I love you. Always know that. You are going to be a great mother. Johnny is lucky to have you. As long as he treats you and the baby good I will stay away. Your happiness will always be my happiness. Just know that. " Then he walked off.

As he disappeared in the distance I wondered if I lost him forever. Would I ever see him again? How could I go again without his kisses, without his warmth? I fell to my knees and bawled my eyes out. The pain was so bad. Life was so cruel. Just when we could finally be together. I mean the baby was a miracle, a blessing that I did not regret. I just wished it was Jax's child. The timing was so off. I never avoided having kids it just had never happened before. Why now?

When I finally made it home my eyes where red and puffy from so much crying. I was feeling like a part of me died. I opened the door, Jax came running to me. I patted his head, hugged him remembering how he and Jax had played together.

"Oh Jax. I love you so much"

"And me? Do you love me so much?" I looked up and there he was.

15 NEW BEGINNINGS

There he was. Johnny standing right behind Jax. He helped me up and looked at me with a worried look.

"Kate, what's wrong? Are you ok?"

I started to cry again. It was that deep type of cry like when someone close to you dies. He hugged me and I just cried in his shoulder. He had no idea. He held me and just let me cry because that was the type of guy he was. He was a wonderful guy. He was the best friend anyone could have. But he wasn't Jax.

After a few minutes, I told that I needed a moment alone. I had to take a shower and then we would talk.

"I'm worried." He said, "Go ahead I will be right here waiting."

I tried to smile. I hopped in the shower got into my pajamas. When Johnny came looking for me I had fallen asleep in the bed before I could even head back downstairs. He did not know what kind of day I had had. He could not even imagine, not in all his wildest dreams. He was innocent and that made it hurt much more. He jumped into bed, hugged me and fell asleep as well.

That night Jax was in my dreams. I was dreaming that he was the one I shared my life with and that the baby was his baby. I was extremely happy. Maybe this happiness was not possible. It would be too perfect and perfect is something that is not possible for a lifetime. You can have a perfect moment but not a perfect lifetime. In my dream Jax was holding this baby boy and looking at me with a look of pride and love. It was pure joy.

When I woke up I realized it was just a dream. Instantly the pain came back. The realization of what was happening was too much to handle. I felt my tummy and remembered that I had a baby in there. I looked around and smelled an aroma that got my stomach grumbling. Johnny had breakfast ready for me. I looked at him and smiled. He was not Jax but he was my very best friend. He deserved to be happy and I had to realize that this would be a new life. I had to focus on our future and know that I was one lucky girl, I just had to keep telling myself that.

"Johnny, you are so good to me. I don't deserve you. I don't know if I make you happy or not. You are my best friend."

"Of course, you make me happy! You are my dream girl! I need to know Kate, what is going on. Did the doctors find something wrong with you or the vet with Jax? Maybe I should have not left you back by yourself. Please tell me."

"They did find something. Something big. Something amazing. They found a baby."

He screamed out of joy. Picked me up and twirled me around. He was so happy and all I could picture was Jax's broken hearted face. Jax's tears. Johnny's happiness was Jax's doom. One could not come without the other.

"Now I understand. You are hormonal. You are pregnant! This is the best news I have ever heard. You have made me so happy! We are going to be a true family. Jax will soon have someone to play with!"

"That's good, you deserve to be happy. That is all I want"

"Kate, I will make a good dad, the best. I promise"

"I don't doubt it. By the way it's a boy."

"Isn't it too early to tell?"

"Yes, but a little birdie already told me. It's a boy. "

Johnny had so much to say. He went on and on about everything we needed to do to prepare for our baby. I just zoned out. My new life had just started. My new life without Jax. Again, I had to face a life without him. Again, I had to build another life. This little baby had replaced him I have heard that a mothers love is great and now I know it is true because all ready without meeting my son I loved him so much that I said bye to my soulmate in order to have the best life for him.

I now had a new soulmate.

The days flew by. I had submerged myself into my work and into getting ready for my baby boy. I stopped taking jobs out of town. Every time Johnny would go I found myself going to the park where I had met with Jax. I would sit there and think about him. I felt his presence there. Sometimes I would feel his eyes from afar on me. I'm not sure if this was all in my head but it gave me comfort. I looked out to the duckpond. The days where colder and the ducks where gone, my belly was growing. I was changing and Jax wasn't here to see that.

I wondered where Jax was. Did he go back to his planet? Did he stay here? I could picture him here walking around feeling sad. Would he meet someone else too? Eventually he probably would. I hated to think about that. Anyone would fall head over heels for him. She would be so fortunate. I hated her. I hated someone I did not even know. I wanted to be her. She would be getting his kisses, she would be in his arms. She would be the one looking into his eyes.

What I hated more is to think that he would be looking into her eyes. Holding her. Stretching out his hand and it not being my hands landing on his. Would he love her? Would he forget me? This was unbearable to go through and yet I knew this was exactly what I was putting Jax through. How he had to be hurting.

I started to walk back to my car when all of a sudden I saw him. He was far away from me. His blonde hair, his blue eyes looking at me. Then he got into a car and disappeared. He was here! So close. I wanted to run to him. He was here feeling the same way as me I was sure. We were breathing the same air. I smiled, I think I just realized he would never be out of my life. He would always be a part of it even if it was from afar. My impossible love. My lost boy. So close yet so far.

I was still his. He was still mine. No matter where life took us or with who. Every so often I would feel his look. He was always with me. I knew he was watching me from a distance. I always looked around and from time to time I would catch a glimpse of those sad blue eyes or of his blonde hair. My boy, my blonde, blue eyed boy.

16 ALEXANDER

The day finally came. The baby was coming. Johnny was prepared. He had planned for months for this day. We got to the hospital and a few hours later Alexander came to our lives. He was the most perfect little boy. Dark black hair and to my surprise blue eyes. Blue eyes that reminded me of Jax. I had no clue why he had blue eyes. I had no blue eyes in my family and neither did Johnny. I stared and stared into his eyes feeling perplexed.

Our families came. Our coworkers came. Everyone commented on those eyes. This little guy had my heart. Such a little miracle looking back at me. Johnny could not be any prouder. After two days we were dismissed. My parents stayed with us for a few days. They helped me out with Xander. After they left I thought to myself that now my new life with my new family started.

The first few months consisted of bottle feeding, changing diapers and burping this little guy. Xander was his nickname. Jax, our dog took to him right away and everywhere Xander was Jax would be close by. Johnny started to work again. I decided to work from home. I would not take as many jobs as before but I was okay with this. All of a sudden Xander was my priority and my goals had changed. Becoming a mommy consumed me and I was ok with it.

One of the nights Johnny was out, Xander could not stop crying. He was acting very colicky and would not fall asleep. I rocked him, I gave him the bottle and I burped him. He cried and cried. It was a hot night he was about 6 months now. I went to the back yard to let Jax out and get some fresh air with Xander. Maybe that would soothe him. It was now evening time and the night was refreshing. The sun had set and it felt so peaceful to sit and feel the cool air. Xander calmed down. I took the car seat with me and placed him there. I rocked him for a while and sang a few nursery songs that I had recently memorized. He soon fell asleep. My little angel was sleeping peacefully.

I was just going to pick him up to head back inside when I heard a sound and looked up. There he was.

Jax.

My heart stopped.

Is this the way we would always meet!?

"Hi my darling."

"Hi." I had no words. What did this mean? Why was he back?

"Oh Kate" he grabbed me, pulled me close and said, "Tell me it's ok, tell me this is ok" then he kissed me and then he stopped.

"It's ok." I then grabbed him and kissed him. Here we were together again. The moon was out, the stars were out and they were our witness of how profound our love was. I did not want to pull away but I had to and it took every energy left inside of me to do so.

"Jax, what are you doing here?"

He then looked over to Xander.

"I came to meet him. He is a part of you and I had to see him. I mean if that is ok with you of course."

At that moment Jax, our dog ran to him, licking him like he knew him. He jumped on him and they played for a bit. He then walked over to Xander and just then Xander opened his eyes.

Jax quickly looked at me.

"His eyes!"

"I know. I don't know how, but he has your eyes!"

Jax gave him a kiss on his forehead then headed towards me.

"You are a part of me and so Xander is a part of me too, we are all connected. Even Xander in a way." He smiled liking the fact that Xander resembled him.

"Every morning I get to see you when I see my son and his bright blue eyes. It is the most painful reminder and the most beloved gift that I have."

"I should go." Jax said softly. "I don't even know if I should have come in the first place."

I quickly grabbed his hand. It was instinct. I did not want him to leave. After all this time I needed a little more time with him. I ached for him again. My body and soul needed him, wanted him. All those feelings were suddenly awakened.

"Jax."

"It's ok I'm fine."

But he wasn't fine. I saw it in his eyes. I heard it in his voice. He had lost weight. He had a painful look in his eyes. He was sad, as sad as I was but worse because at least I had Xander. He really did not have anyone. He was alone. My heart went out to him. I wish I could comfort him. I wanted to give him hope and make him feel better. What I wanted to say was that it was going to be ok, instead I just looked down unable to say what my heart was screaming.

"Are you doing ok?" he asked.

"No, no Jax I'm not. Each day is a battle but now I have Xander and he helps me through it. I hurt. I miss you. I look for you in everything. I look for you everywhere. I need you. No, I am not fine but I am trying. What choice do I have? These are the cards that life has dealt me, dealt us."

"Just know I will always be around. Just like that day in the park. I may not be next to you. But I will be there from afar. I miss you."

"I know, I feel you there. I miss you too."

"I should go. Take care of Xander he is worth everything. He is what is most important now. That little part of you that is more precious than life itself. I will hold on to that."

Xander started to fuss. I went to pick him up and when I turned around Jax was gone. Every time he left my life he left such a big gap in my heart. Not even Xander could fill that gap. It was a part of my heart and soul that just belonged to Jax. I then looked at my little boy and my heart filled with love for him. He was so innocent and Jax was right Xander was worth everything. He was the one thing that kept me going. For him I would accept my destiny. I picked up my baby and headed back inside feeling a little lost but knowing that I had to find my way.

......8 Years Later......

Time passed and I thought Jax would be showing up again. He didn't. I looked for him at the park. I sat out in the back yard but no Jax. The days flew by and life continued on. Xander became the center of my world. Xander was now eight years old. He had grown to be a wonderful son. He loved to play baseball. He loved his father and he loved Jax, our dog. Jax was not doing so well lately. He had grown old and had a bone disease he was suffering through. Jax still followed Xander everywhere. My two sweet babies.

Johnny was now our main provider. I eventually had become a full time housewife. I loved it. Just as much as I had loved being a journalist years back. I led a comfortable life. I could not complain. My day would consist of caring for my family. Xander brought so much love and joy. He filled my days and kept me pretty busy.

I was very proud of how wonderful he was. Johnny was an excellent father and helped out with him as much as he could. He was not the type of dad that had to be told to do stuff he simply would do what was needed and did it joyfully. I appreciated him a lot. He never found out about Jax. There were times it felt like Jax never existed. A day or two would pass without me thinking about him but then boom something would bring him to my thoughts and the memories would rush back to me.

Today was a family day for us. We had breakfast to-gether and enjoyed each other's daily stories. Xander felt happy with his two parents and his best friend, Jax. We then hopped into our car and took off to one of Xander's base-ball games. We were almost there. When out of nowhere a big truck lost control. The truck ended up in our lane. Our car turned and turned. The truck fell over. Our car was crushed. Everything went black.

17 SACRIFICE (JAX)

All these years I had been living a quiet life. I found a job in an adoption agency and I have to admit I had a very satisfying job. I matched homeless children up with families. I myself did not have a family so I found comfort and joy watching as the children would find a home and people that loved them like every kid deserves. I think everyone needs someone to love and to be loved. My family was Kate. Although I did meet a few ladies that had shown interest in me I just couldn't reciprocate the feelings. They would flirt and say comments hinting that they liked me but I never paid attention. I did not even like the attention. I tried to focus on my job. I laid low on the social life. I don't know if I would ever be able to move on I just knew that for now it was not even a possibility in my heart.

I lived in a one bedroom apartment about 20 miles from Kate. I was very careful for her to not see me. It was just less painful this way for the both of us. I sometimes got to see Xander. Some days Kate did not go to his games and I would attend. I even spoke to him a few times. I thought to myself what a great kid he was. How I wished he was my kid. I also observed Johnny. I had to admit he was a good man. I had to step aside. He was good to both of them. As long as he treated them like that I would not interfere. They made a nice family. I learned to love them from afar. Johnny, I respected. I would also see Kate from a distance. I could tell that sometimes she would be looking around as if she was searching for me. Our love had not died out.

She still sat in her backyard during the evenings and went to the park every once in a while. Sometimes with Xander, most times by herself, never with Johnny. She would sit for hours some days. It was one of the hardest things for me to see her and not be able to approach her. I couldn't though. I knew it would just make things more painful for the both of us. Seeing each other and not being able to touch or kiss would be unbearable. So I stayed away. I did it for her and for Xander.

One day out of the blue I felt this sharp pain. What was this anguish I was feeling in my chest? Everything around me went dark and suddenly I knew. Kate. She needed me. She was in trouble. I had to get to her. Oh, dear God, please let her be ok. I was sitting on my couch watching TV. I turned it off rode around her house, the park and everywhere I could think of. I had no clue where she could be at. Her car was missing along with Xander and Johnny. I went back home and started to call police stations and hospitals. I prayed that I did not find her through one of these calls. My prayer that day was not heard.

I rushed to find her. I researched and found out she had been in a terrible accident. She was in the hospital. Johnny and Xander were fine. Kate not so much. My Kate I had to get there. I finally made it. I ran to the waiting room. I saw them. Jonny and Xander. What could I say? How could I approach them? I was nobody to them. I sat and pretended I was there for someone else. I saw a concerned look on Johnny's face and that worried me. Later her parents arrived and they were hysterical. I started to pace. I sat closer to them so I could eavesdrop on their conversations. I needed to know.

Finally, I saw a doctor come out and he told them she was in a coma. They did what they could now it was up to her. Basically, the longer she was in a coma the harder it would be to come out of this ok. Kate's parents decided to take Xander home. Johnny stayed. I was not sure what to do. I decided to give it a couple of days and see. I needed to think. It was the most difficult thing to go back to my apartment and wait without knowing what was happening.

The days passed and her condition stayed the same. No improvement was the only news the doctors had for Johnny and her family. I was coming to the end of my rope. My patience was quickly wearing off. I had sacrificed enough. I had sacrificed my love. I would not sacrifice Kate. I had to step in. Johnny had to know. Enough was enough. It was time.

"Excuse me but I really need to talk to you." I approached Johnny cautiously at the waiting room. Xander or her parents were not there so I thought this would be the perfect time to talk to him man to man.

"Umm, do I know you?" he asked.

"No but I know you and most of all I know Kate." He looked confused, I could not blame him.

"Who are you?"

"My name is Jax."

"What? That is my dog's name. Is this a joke?" "No, it's not."

"What I'm about to tell you is going to change your world. I want to start off my saying. I was never going to step in. I had stepped aside."

"What are you talking about?"

"Kate is my soulmate. She is the love of my life. We first met when we were teenagers. Please sit down this will be a lot to take in. It was a lot for Kate the first time we met. Please hear me out. I am the only one that can help her. She placed her happiness aside once before to make you happy. She sacrificed. I sacrificed. Now you need to sacrifice. If you truly love her, this is the only way to save her."

"Are you nuts? Look if this is a joke, it is not very funny. I have my wife here and I don't know if I am about to lose her."

"No, please hear me out. This is definitely not a joke. This is about Kate. This is about saving her. I know how this will sound to you but I promise you it's all true. I can prove it. Listen to me and at the end I will show you the proof and then you can decide for yourself. I just need about twenty minutes or so."

"Fine, I need a coffee break anyway, lets go to the cafeteria."

As I started telling him everything, and I do mean everything from the start I could almost feel his insides as he came to the realization that his life was not what he had thought it was. His wife who was so dear to him belonged to him as the woman by his side but belonged to me in every way that truly mattered. She belonged to me in her soul. She longed to be with me. Now he understood many things that were not so clear and they started to make sense. Jax his dog. The day he got home and she had been crying so hard. It was not because she was pregnant it was due to the fact that she had decided to give up Jax. Her trips to the park. How she would sit in the back yard for hours sometimes.

I told him about the meetings and about how I had decided to vanish from her life. I then explained that in order to save her I had to take her to my planet. I could save her there. If he would let me she would live. Kate would return to him, to me, to us, to Xander. If he refused she could die and then leave Xander with no mother. It would be his choice. Could he be willing to give up Kate and sacrifice like we had sacrificed years ago? Was his love for her as strong as ours? We would soon find out.

I grabbed Johnny's hand and closed my eyes. Johnny then saw visions of Kate and I. I imagine how strong this must be for him. I even sympathized. How crazy was this life that I had to sit here tonight, face to face with my...... I wouldn't say enemy more like my......rival. Johnny shed a couple of tears as he realized I was telling him the truth.

I knew what he was feeling. I could understand. We both loved her. Did he love her enough to let her go?

Johnny stayed sitting down stunned for a little while. Then he looked at me and responded,

"Take her. She is everything to me. Take her and save her."

I did not see any hesitation or doubt when he spoke. He proved that night that he definitely loved her as much as I loved her. My respect for him grew and I understood why Kate respected and cared for this man. He was honorable. I could not bring myself to hate him as much as I wanted to. I felt bad but at this point there was no choice. It had to be done. He had to know the truth. It was time.

"Thank you. I'm sorry it had to be this way." I held out my hand and we shook hands. I started to walk away.

"Jax."

"Yeah?"

"Bring her back safe. " Johnny said with his eyes full of tears, heartbroken. It was a feeling I was very familiar with except that this time it was worse because it was Kate's life on the line.

I nodded in agreement. I went in to Kate's room and saw her there lying down attached to all kinds of human machines. She looked pale as she lied there so still. Her arms were all bruised up and filled with cuts. Ohhh Kate. I would save you. I had to. There was no way I would lose you. I leaned in softly whispered,

"Kate it's me, Jax. Hang on my love, hang on"

I was back and this time I could not let her down. I would not lose her. She was everything. I grabbed her and off we went.

18 AVIAN

There was darkness all around me. I was alone. It was cold. I don't know how long I had been like this. Something felt strange but at the same time comforting. Where was I? All of a sudden I saw a light. It warmed me up. I felt....complete. I felt....whole.

I opened my eyes and I saw him. It was Jax. He was sitting next to my side holding my hand. Jax! Jax! Was this a dream? Where was I? Something felt different. What was happening? Did I die? Was I in heaven?

"Jax." I tried to talk but it came out muffled.

"Shhhh, I'm here. You are going to be ok." Jax was sitting next to me holding my hand and stroking my hair.

I was in a white room. It was warm and bright here. Everything smelled clean like the smell of clean laundry. I was not hooked up to any machines but there was a monitor on the wall with all my information on it. I could see my heartbeat, blood pressure and all my vitals digitalized. How could that be if I was not connected to anything? I looked at Jax looking for an explanation. He gave me the brightest smile. Then I focused on his eyes, oh God his beautiful eyes. Then I quickly thought of Xander.

"Xander....Johnny.... what happened? Are they ok?" A flush of visions came to me. Baseball game....car.... accident... My heart rate went up.

"Shhhh, calm down they are good. They are at home safe and sound. Don't worry my love I will explain every-thing but for now just rest. You need to rest to get stronger."

I trusted him. I trusted him with my life. Just then I fell right back in a deep sleep. I had been given medications so that I could come out of my coma little by little. I needed the information to be spoon fed so that it would not be too much too soon. I just was not aware. I could not have imagined what had just transpired. Not in my wildest dreams would I have guessed that I had just traveled across space and time to now visit his world.

..........weeks later..........

"Slowly honey." Jax told me as he helped in into what was in his world a vehicle. Except it was different. This "car" was silent. Apparently these vehicles did not run out of gas. They ran out of energy. Not sure I understood how. I got in and the ride was so smooth. The car drove itself. As soon as Jax told it where to go, it took off.

I looked around at this new world, this new universe, Avian they called it. It was like out of a movie. I looked up at what would be the sky in our world and here it was white. Completely white like a giant cloud. Farther in the sky they had two medium size suns and you could see two more planets beyond them. This was truly incredible. The stars seemed closer, bigger and you could see them in the daylight.

The music playing softly in the car was soothing. Jax held his arm around me. His face was gleaming with joy. We passed by lots of homes. These homes had clean lines. Everywhere I looked was clean. All the trees were trimmed. The grass on all the yards were green. The people here were all dressed in lightly colored clothes. They all had decent haircuts and no one stuck out. They looked content.

"Is everyone happy here?"

"For the most part, yeah, some more than others though. I am very, very happy right now!" Jax laughed.

I smiled. Us driving to his home seemed to be the most natural, normal thing. It felt good. I think this is how it was supposed to be from the start. I closed my eyes and drifted off. I felt for the first time in my life that I belonged. I felt safe. I was happy. I had no worries. This was my world. This was my boy. This was real and I was alive.

Finally, we drove up to one of the homes. We entered and as soon as I stepped in it felt familiar somehow. I felt at home.

"Welcome home my darling" He then swooped me up and carried me inside just like just married couples did in the movies.

Jax showed me around. He was like a little boy at Christmas time. Running from room to room looking to see if I had approved of how his home looked. I thought it was perfect. Everything had a place and nothing was out of it. This was his real home and now I was here, with him! All of a sudden I realized we were completely alone. We were not out in public. We were totally alone in our home. No judgments, nowhere to hide, nowhere to run, nowhere to disappear to.

I think Jax realized this too. For the first time since I met him he seemed nervous and unsure of what to do next. That made him even more attractive. He started to caress my neck. Gently stroking it while looking into my eyes. Then he started to rub my arm. We started kissing. He grabbed me in his arms and took me to the bedroom. His bed that looked as soft as a cloud. Finally, we started to make love. I had always been his spiritually and emotionally and now I was his physically as well. It was an outer body experience. All my senses came alive and I was his. Completely his and he was mine. After it was over I fell asleep in his arms. I had never slept better in my life.

I woke up the next day and Jax was not next to me. I quickly went to the bathroom and saw that he had bought me everything I could need and more! I saw a toothbrush, toothpaste, lotions, shampoos, more than enough. I knew what they were but because everything had one simple label on the bottles. I took the toothpaste and brushed my teeth. The quality of the toothpaste was really incredible. I felt all my mouth super fresh, just like if I just had a cleaning done. I had to take out some lotion and try it out. It went on so creamy. It smelled like vanilla and lavender. My skin felt like I just came out of a spa. I quickly understood that here everything was luxurious. I couldn't wait to find out more about this world because so far, I loved it.

"Jax, where are you? 'I called to my sweetheart.

"I'm here." He yelled from the living room.

He was sitting with some kind of tablet punching in buttons.

"I am ordering us food. Here in Avian we just tell this tablet what we want and someone shows up with it in about an hour or so. You can order pretty much anything you want. "

"Really! Just like that! I have so much to learn. How do you pay the person? Do you use a credit card or something."

"We don't pay. We don't use money. Here everyone has a job. As you are growing up you are assigned a job according to your abilities and likes. Your job can change as you get older. You work in your community, you go to church, you are a good citizen. In exchange, you eat, you receive medical attention, you get a good home, a car and you live comfortably. It works out. There are no social classes here. Everyone is equal. The man who picks up the garbage makes the same as a doctor and is respected in the same way. "

"Wow, that sounds wonderful. What if someone doesn't want their job, they refuse it or disobey? Are there any laws or consequences?"

"But of course. We have leaders. They are the elders. Those elderly people you saw when you connected to me on earth are the elders. They do not come from our planet. They have the last word. I disobeyed when I snuck off to earth remember! I had to pay by staying here for a few years and learning patience. They give you a consequence according to what you have done. I have heard stories of people that have committed bad crimes and they had been banished from our world. Where do they take them, I do not know. It keeps our world in the condition it is in. No one has a reason to complain. Some get demoted to the jobs no one wants and if you do good you get better jobs. We also get to observe other planets like yours and can clearly see how good we have it. We don't have any wars. Our planet is healthy, we live very long lives and we follow the rules."

"Makes sense."

I smiled. This was a wonderful place and now I was part of it. "Soooo, about last night!"

"Oohhhh my love, you are tempting me!!!"

We smiled and our loved consumed us. We gave into our passion and gave each other completely to one another once again. I felt that I had literally died and gone to heaven. Now I understood what that phrase meant!

19 TOMORROW

The days passed and my body got stronger. I had completely healed. I was used to living here in Avian. Jax and I were living as a couple. It was Nirvana. We woke up together each morning and we explored his world. He explained to me how this world worked. I met people from here and they were all so nice. The kind of people you want as friends. They made me feel welcomed. We were invited to their homes and I got to observe how they lived. They were loving to one another.

I was so mesmerized by the way Avian's lived their lives. They were amazing. They lived in harmony. Every person of the community was valued and respected, even children. Love filled their lives. They were beautiful on the inside and on the outside. I admired them and wanted to fit in.

Each day was a treat. I felt part of a real community in which everyone knew each other and helped one another out. I could easily live here. Earth was so different. We earthly humans had a lot to learn. For fun Avians pretty much did a lot of the same things we did. They loved to get together. They loved sports and games and they loved to study other worlds. It was like watching TV for humans. They would turn on their screens which to me was like a big TV and they could tune in to earth and other planets. Like watching national geographic! Amazing. I actually got to see other humans, other aliens. Most looked human. A lot of other human races are taller and more beautiful than we are. Some are not as evolved and at least I know we are somewhere in the middle. God is at the center of all this but we cannot see him unless he himself lets himself be seen. That is just how it is. He is everywhere and he is nowhere but his presence is known throughout all the universes out there. Every world has a story to tell. Their own bibles and their own religions. There is not enough time to take it all in. I was just getting my first peek into it all and it is very overwhelming.

"Jax do you have any family?"

Jax bowed his head down.

"No, my parents went on a mission to another planet and the spaceship actually had a malfunction. It exploded, they never made it back alive. "

"Oh, I'm sorry to hear that."

"How about your job. What is your job here in Avian?"

"I have been granted time off from my job here on Avian. On earth, I was given a mission to work as a helper. I was working connecting orphans children with families. You see we may request jobs on other planets that need help. I did it to be near you. Here in Avian my job is like a guide. I still work with the youth. I am expected to talk to them and act as a mentor. You see, on earth some children have good mentors, others not so much. It is a big factor in shaping a child's future. Children need to have good values taught to them and need to be surrounded by good role models. I am one of them. I can act like a big brother to them. I am like a teacher in some ways. I take them to sport games, when parents can't. I form friendships and counsel them. They feel they always have someone to turn to besides their parents and therefore grow up to be stable citizens. Teachers of every sort are very valuable. In our world, we acknowledge that. I am a called a big brother. Kind of like the big brother, big sister program that you have on earth."

"This is all so very interesting. I am proud of you. You have such a kind heart. You amaze me Jax, the more I learn about you the more I admire you."

"Jax, do I belong here?" I need to know.

I had to know. What was my place? Did I fit in this world? In his world?

Jax did not respond.

"Jax, where is my place? Can other humans from other worlds live here, is that allowed?"

"No."

"What! No?"

"You are a special case. You are here simply because we got matched and this is the first case of having soulmates in different worlds. This is a first in history and so the elders allowed this exception. See Kate when I tell you that you are special I really do mean it!" Jax joked.

He tried to make light of the situation but it worried me. What did this mean? Would we be separated again? What would happen now?

"There are no rules for this, it had never happened before. I came in front of the elders begging them to allow me to bring you here. Once long ago they had denied my request. There is a certain order to the universe and we have to let humans evolve at their pace. Once you had your accident it was different because it was now life or death so once again I went before the elders. This time they approved your stay."

"So, what now? I have a son, Jax." then I added quietly "and a husband."

"I know." Jax bowed his head, his tone changed. "You have decisions to make or should I say we because I am here with you to help you in any way I can. I cannot tell you what to do but I can support you. Once a long time ago you made a decision for the both of us. I will tell you the same thing I told you before I will respect and understand whatever you decide. I know you have a pure heart. I wish we could stay here and live just like we have been these past few days. I could dig out the courage to probably argue a good case to see if the elders could approve you living here but that leaves the issue of Xander. I could even try for him to come but then he would be separated from his dad so they most likely will not approve for Xander to come. This is not an easy case."

"There is also the fact that I cheated on him. This time it changes everything. I was unfaithful. It doesn't feel like cheating though because how could it be cheating to be with the one you are meant to be with? Maybe the one I was really cheating on was you, Jax. I cheated on you too!"

This was all so confusing. My world was flipped. My head pinned and the more I thought about it the more I knew that I had to face my life. It was time to say good bye to this dream world that I had been living for the past few months.

"I don't know what to say. All I can say is that you are my world. I don't belong to Avian, I belong to you. We belong to each other. Home is wherever you are. I want to tell you to stay with me. To pick me. I want to tell you that I am the right choice. At the same time I understand that Johnny and Xander exist. They are real. I got to meet Johnny at the hospital and he truly does love you. He let me take you. After everything I told him, he risked losing you to me in order for you to live. That says a lot to me. Then there is Xander. There is not right solution. I'm sorry I wish I could say that I have an answer but I don't. What does your heart tell you to do?"

"My heart! My heart tells me to grab on to you and never let you go. My heart tells me you are the one over and over again. I want to live this life. The one I have here in Avian with you. I was born in the wrong planet. I belong here."

This was all the honest truth.

"The next flight to earth leaves in two days, after that it will be a very long time until the next one. It could be years even."

"I have lots to think about. Jax do you thing you can do something for me? Can you give me today? Can I have now? Can I just have today?"

"What do you have in mind?"

"I want today. I want to live out our dreams and our fantasies. I want today to be unforgettable, for it to be a day we create forever memories. Let's go. Let's go live. Take me wherever you want and let's just love each other. Tomorrow is another day. I don't have to decide today. Today I want to live. Today I am Avian." I spoke with excitement. "I want to be Kate from Avian today. Jax's Kate. I want to be in your arms, by your side with no worries. The problems will be here tomorrow waiting for us. "

Jax loved the idea. He quickly put on his big, beautiful smile. So that is just what we did. Jax grabbed my hand and took me to a place that had a field full of flowers. The fragrance was heavenly. We were in the middle of forest like place. There was a lake and next to it the field of flowers. We took a blanket he had packed and laid it out right in the middle of it. He had planned the whole thing. We were going to have a romantic picnic. We talked, we laughed we loved each other. In that moment, in that day we were us. We were Kate and Jax. We were together and the rest did not matter.

The rest we would face together, but not today. Today we laughed. Today we loved each other. Today Jax and I were one. We were lovers. Today we had a real date. We held each other, caressed each other, kissed and simply enjoyed being like this. We did not know exactly how tomorrow would unfold or what the future had in store for us but today, today life was good. Life in Avian had been remarkable. I felt Avian. For Jax to leave this amazing planet and come live on earth to watch me from afar when we were split up spoke volumes about his great love for me. Today was a day that I would forever treasure. And tomorrow, tomorrow was another day.

20 EARTH

"Ready?" Jax looked at me.

Here we stood back on earth. I was back home now. Jax and I sat in the rental car looking at my house wondering what the future would bring us. My house seemed so unfamiliar and so distant to me now. I had so many memories here and yet they felt like they belonged to someone else. This was not a part of the new life I wanted. I left earth not knowing that that girl who left would never come back.

I wanted to scream. To say no and tell Jax to take me back to Avian. That was what I wanted but there was no way I could leave Xander. As much as I loved Jax, I loved Xander just as strong but in a different way. A mothers love is so great that it will always come second to her children. That is just how it goes. My Xander had to come first. The pull of my love as a mother attached me to earth. It grounded me to my son and that could never change.

"I will never be ready but here we go." Jax held my hand. I smiled and looked at our hands together. "Never let go Jax, don't let go of me ever."

"I have to give you time and space. Take as much as you need to take. When you are ready meet me at the park same time as we use to meet. I will be there waiting."

Jax spoke with a shaky voice. I felt how his hand trembled when he let go of my hand. He did not even have to tell me how he felt because it was the same sadness I was feeling. To leave his side and peel myself away from him was like ripping myself in half. I got out of the car looked back and saw him drive away. I almost thought of running after the car. I could not get Jax's look that he had on his face as he was driving off out of my mind. All I could think about was that Jax was leaving. He was driving away and leaving me behind and I did not know for how long. After being with him for so long, knowing his face was the first face I would see in the morning and now knowing I would not have him there was so hard. How many times would I suffer this fate?

I walked to my front door and knocked. What would life be like now? I was back but I was not the same. This new Kate had gone a transformation inside and out. I cut my hair off. I styled in straight now, I was dressed in light colored clothes and I had lost a few pounds. I had come back from a deathbed. The accident had not left any physical marks in me they were all on the inside.

There was no way life could go back to what it used to be like. I had been gone for a while. It had been 8 months from the time Jax took me from the hospital. The door opened and the first thing I saw was those big blue eyes.

"Mom!" Xander jumped on me "Mom, you're back! You're ok mom!"

"Yes, my son, I am back. Xander, oh Xander I love you so much"

I walked in and saw Johnny standing there looking at me like he had just seen a ghost. His face went white.

"Hi Johnny." I looked at him and was not sure how to act around him. We always had such a comfortable relationship. Now for the first time it felt awkward. Just knowing that he now knew everything changed things between us. Well, he knew almost everything because he didn't know exactly what had happened during the past few months and now it was my turn to fill him in.

"Mom, mom I missed you mom. I want you to know I have been a good boy while you were gone. I have good grades all A's and B's. My team did not make the championship but we played good and strong. Dad said it doesn't matter because we had fun and that's what matters."

"Honey, I'm so sorry I missed your games. I'm sure you did great and your dad is right as long as you had fun that is all that matters. I am so proud of you. Stand here and let me look at you!"

I was not sure how Johnny explained my absence to him and to everybody else for that matter. So I needed to be careful with my words with him until I was in the loop.

"It's ok mom you are back and now you won't miss any more games. Everything can go back to the way it used to be right?"

He hugged me tightly. He needed reassurance from me. I was not sure what to say. I had to be careful not to make any promises that I would not be able to keep. I looked up at Johnny and he gave me a look of confusion. He looked tired. He normally would have ran to hug me and now he just stood there not knowing what to do or what to say.

"Xander, I don't want you to worry I am back. I am healthy and I won't leave you ever again. You are stuck with me"

"Ok mom." After what seemed like 100 questions from him, he finally felt satisfied, he took a shower and went to bed. I felt so bad. He really needed to feel safe. He needed to believe that he would not lose me again. He hugged me and did not want to let me go just like I did not want to let him go. My sweet little boy, I was so happy to have him back. He was the one person that I left everything for. He was the one person that was my anchor. I love him so much and he would never know how much.

"There is food in the kitchen if you are hungry." Johnny offered to break the tension between us.

"Ummm, Yeah sure."

We walked to the kitchen and he served me some leftover spaghetti he had made earlier. I had to get used to eating normal food again. Food high in calories and sugar but was also yummy.

"Thank you Johnny."

"It's nothing I had cooked earlier today..."

"No, that is not what I mean." I interrupted him. "I mean thank you for saving my life."

"Oh that. Yeah. I mean, I would do anything for you. There was no other choice. What was I going to do?"

"That was really, really admirable. I owe you my life. I just hope you don't hate me."

"No, I don't. You would have done the same for me. You are my best friend. You are my wife."

21 XANDER

It took me a few days to feel ready to talk to Johnny about everything. I finally asked him if when Xander was at school we could sit and have a conversation. I think he knew what was coming. His face said it all.

"Johnny, everything that Jax told you was true. I never told you because I never wanted to hurt you. I did not understand what was happening most of the time myself. Even though I know there is no excuse in the world. I want you to know besides that I had never lied to you about anything."

"Did you ever love me?"

"Yes! I still do and always will love you. I just love you in a different way. You have been amazing with me and amazing with Xander. As a wife, I have no complaints. If I would have met you first everything would have been different but Jax walked into my life and since the first instant I became his. There is nothing I could have done. I tried. I tried to hate him. I wanted to forget him but I didn't. It was so impossible. Even with him not being present physically he was always with me."

"Do I now know everything or are there any more surprises in the future for me? I think I deserve to know, at least give me that."

"It's hard. It's hard because I know by telling you all this I am hurting you and that is the last thing I want to do."

"I need to know. As a friend, I ask you to please just tell me."

"Ok then. You already know Jax took me to Avian. We spent the days there together. Like a couple."

"So, you were together, together."

"Yeah."

"Ok, and now what happens next?"

"I think you know now things can never go back to being the same as they use to. Johnny, I love Jax. I want to be with him. I still want a friendship with you. If that is possible, I mean. We will always be connected because we share Xander." I had to be clear. I did not want to play any games with him or give him false hope. He was right he deserved the truth. Finally, he knew everything.

During the next few days I spent packing up my stuff. I thought it was fair if Johnny kept the house. Jax, our dog I found out had passed away while I was gone. One Jax left my life and the other entered it. I was almost ready except for one important detail, Xander. He had been asking why I was packing and I had been putting it off by telling him that we were going to have a new home but that I would explain later. This time I needed to explain things to him. He was a big boy and knew something was wrong. I felt horrible I hurt Johnny I did not want to hurt my Xander. I took Xander to the same park that I always met with Jax. I did not plan it, without thinking about is as soon as I got in the car this is where I ended up at.

"Xander, you know I love you with all of my heart right?"

"Yeah I know"

"I told you we were going to a new home but it will just be us. You and I. Johnny will stay at the house we live in now. He is not coming with us."

"Why? Why can't dad come?'

"We decided we want to stay best friends, I will have a new apartment and for us and he can visit you as much as he wants to or you want to. You will have two rooms. That means two homes, more toys, two beds, two of everything. You will have the same school, same friends and the same baseball team. That won't change. You are lucky. You will also have the love of both of us. That will never change either."

His little face scrunched up. He gave me his mad face. Maybe it was too much for him.

"But mom I don't want two of everything. I just want two parents, that's it. I don't want to move and I don't want you to move. You already moved and went away for a long time. Now I want you to stay."

"Oh honey, you do have me. That will never change. Johnny and I will always love each other. I will never leave you again. Johnny and I will be together for special events like birthdays, Christmas and stuff like that. You will live with both of us."

"You don't love dad no more? Is that why you went away from us? Is that why you left us?"

"What! NOOOOO! I went away to get better because of the accident, remember. I would never leave you. That big truck hit us. It hit me the hardest and I had to go away to a better hospital so they could help me wake up. I had to go to get better and come back to be with you."

I grabbed my son and held him. Oh god, what was I doing! How could I explain everything to him? He was so innocent in all of this. I stooped down and got down to his eye level. I had to explain to him and make him understand everything but it was not going as I planned or as I hoped.

"Xander, we will move to our new place, and take it day by day ok? Dad can come anytime he wants, you can see him anytime too. Let's try it and see. Please, I need you to know that we all still love each other. It's just that your dad and I love each other more like best friends. I love him like my best friend and not like my husband but I still love him so much. He is a great man, a great dad and a great friend to me. Can you understand this? You are now old enough to know this kind of stuff. Can you try?"

Xander started to cry.

"Mom I don't like it. I want to go home with both of you!"

"Xander, please."

It must have been almost another hour till I got him to calm down and agree to this. Not that he had to but I felt really guilty so I wanted to take each step slowly. I got home feeling defeated that night. As my head hit my pillow I cried myself to sleep feeling like the worst mother ever.

The next day we got in the car and drove to my new apartment. Jax would not be with us yet. I wanted Xander to get used to living with me for a while and once I knew he adapted to this huge transition only then I could introduce Jax into the picture. Once again Jax had to come second. Once again, our love had to wait. We would see each other when Xander was at his dad's or whenever possible but while Xander was with me, he would be my priority.

Xander walked in and I showed him his new room. I had painted it his favorite color, navy blue. I made sure to have all his favorite games and new games that I knew he would like. Everything was brand new, it was a boy's dream bedroom. I set up a bed that had a fort on the bottom. He walked in and immediately started to play with his new video games. I stood at his door and smiled. To be so small and innocent. I hoped I could make it up to him.

That night when I went to bed, with Xander in the room next to mine I felt that maybe everything could eventually fall into place. I wondered if I did the right thing. Jax and I had waited a what felt like a lifetime to be together. We had sacrificed so many times. We hurt Johnny and now Xander. This time it had to turn out differently. I wanted to make it up to Xander and to Jax. I hoped that eventually Johnny would come to forgive me and we could be friends once again, if not for the sake of the friendship we had of many years than for Xander's sake.

He took everything as best as he could. This was so much. My head felt like exploding. I went to the kitchen had a cup of milk and started to think about the days in Avian. Immediately I started to feel calmer. I pictured how Jax and I had loved each other without boundaries and without guilt. I fell asleep like a baby dreaming that we were back there again.

22 HURT

Life had changed a lot in the past years. Xander was now almost 13 years old. He was entering into his teen age years. He had changed a lot and was now very different compared to that little boy that had moved into my apartment those first few months. The change had been rough on him. A lot more than I anticipated. No matter how much I tried or what I said, Xander was angry. His grades dropped, he started to act out. I thought he would adapt and that it would just take getting use to but as time passed it just got worse. All he wanted to do was be with his father. I introduced him to Jax a year later after we moved out of Johnny's home. I thought a year was plenty to adjust to the change. Thinking that Jax was such a charmer and would win him over easily I thought it would be ok, boy was I wrong.

He wanted nothing to do with him. In the beginning, he placed his anger on me and then it was all on Jax. This made life really hard on me. I continually felt the guilt and took it like a punishment. Maybe I deserved his hate. I took him to therapy to see if they could help but nothing seemed to help. When he was with Johnny he acted great. Johnny talked to him and told him to behave when he was with me but he would not listen.

Eventually I agreed to let him go live with Johnny full time and I just got him on weekends. This decision alone killed me. I missed my son. I felt like a bad mom. It was out of my hands at this point. I had no control over him. No matter what Jax and I did, it was never enough. He got to the point that he did not want to come over not even on the weekends. I know made sure it was just him and I. I would take him fun places, I tried to make it special for him. He was good when it was just us two but as soon as we got home he wanted to leave to go with Johnny. My heart could not take this.

Jax felt guilty as well. He even told me once that he understood if I decided to leave him. My Jax like always thinking of me first and putting himself last. I was so torn. Why was happiness always so out of reach for me? I mean, I had even traveled to another universe and united with my soulmate and yet we could not form a happy family here on earth. Xander was always so upset. I wanted him to be happy. I wanted him to be a regular kid. Now that he was becoming a teenager it was even worse. The negative feelings intensified. The tension in our home was unbearable. I was in a depressed mood all the time.

Johnny worried too. He tried to help me as much as he could from his end. He spoke to Xander and told him that he had to respect Jax. We all went to Xander's baseball games and school events. We planned birthdays together. Nothing seemed to work. I was at the end of my rope.

"Xander, we need to talk" I had taken him out for ice cream. It was my weekend with him and he was acting calm.

"Has Jax ever been mean to you?"

"I hate Jax"

"Why? Has he done anything to you?"

"Yes! He took you away from us!"

"No, he didn't we have always been together."

"You disappeared for almost a year then you got back and left dad."

"Xander, that was between your dad and I, and he understood. I never left you! I adore you. I can't live with this any longer. You act like you hate me. Jax and I are together now you have to respect that. Johnny does."

"Mom, I just want to be with dad. I don't want to be with you. I hate you. You want me to love you then come back home!" Xander yelled and ran out.

"Xander, Xander stop."

Xander ran across the street a car almost hitting him.

"You need to make a choice mom. Who do you love more Jax or me? Pick!"

Then he ran home. (to his dad's home). I called Johnny and let him know what had happened. Johnny said he would talk to him. What else could he do. Inside of me I felt like this was all my fault. Had I acted selfish because I stayed so long in Avian or because I enjoyed my stay there? Was that my mistake? Did I introduce Jax too soon? I tried to recall the moment where I could have done something differently.

When I made it home Jax could hardly understand what I was saying. I was crying so hard I could not talk. Jax sat me down, hugged me and waited till I as calm enough to talk.

"He hates me!" I cried "My son hates me!"

"Kate, he hates *me*." Jax replied

"I can't take this. I can't take his anger any more. It has been years since I left Johnny, he should be over it by now. I did this to him, it's my fault. I lost my sweet little boy. I lost him forever."

"Jax, I tried talking to him, I really did. He would not listen. He wants me to choose you or him! He is just a kid I can't have a kid tell me what to do. He needs to accept and respect you. As wonderful as you have been to both of us. How can he act like this? Where does he get this from? Is he right? Is this all my fault?"

"You are a good mom, don't ever doubt that."

"I just don't know what else to say, what else to do? I think I lost him."

I started to cry again, uncontrollably. I sobbed into Jax's shoulder until I had exhausted all my energy.

I don't remember how I got to bed last night. Jax must have carried me up. I do remember him giving me a glass of milk. I slept soundly. When I woke up I still felt that deep pain in my heart that only a mother can feel when there is a problem with one of her children. I could not be at peace without being at peace with Xander. I could not be happy without knowing Xander was happy. As a mother that is just the way it works. A man's love even if it is your soulmate cannot fill the space of a child's. A mother's love is at another level because this love is not selfish, it is not to do what is best for you but what is best for your child. Your child's happiness comes first, period. I just realized what I had to do. Just then Jax walked in and just by looking at him I could tell he knew me so much that he knew what I needed to do probably before I myself did.

"Kate, the last two times you had to pick I did not say anything I just let you decide. This time it's different you know you have to do it and I understand."

He sat down on the edge of the bed put his hands on his face and just sobbed.

We held each other in grief. He did not deserve this. He had tried so hard to make everything work. It was not his fault and now here he was stepping aside again for the love he had for me and for Xander. Even if Xander had this hate for him, Jax loved this boy. He had no children and this was the child he never had. Even after all the hurtful comments from Xander, Jax loved him and that made me love him even more. Now here I was again in a dilemma that we had to make decisions putting our love aside for others. Our love that was so pure and so huge because with time it had grown and grown had to suffer once again.

23 SHADOW (JAX)

The day Kate went to talk to Johnny I felt that my life came to an end. I had done everything in my power to win Xander over. Nothing worked. He did not let me get close enough to win him over. If I invited him to a baseball game, he would not take of his headphones to talk to me. If we ate dinner at home, he took it to his room. If I bought him a present, he would not want it. I tried and tried. The more that Xander pulled away the more Kate fell apart. I thought by giving it time things would eventually get better. Years passed and it got worse.

Kate would cry at night when she thought I was not listening or I was already asleep. My darling. We were finally together. We went to bed and I got to hold her all night long. I got to see her sweet face every morning. I went to work in the morning and when I got home she greeted me with the biggest smile and had my dinner waiting for me. She loved being a housewife but she also started to write books. She was really good at it. She had published two books already. I was so proud of her.

We had everything. Everything except Xander's approval of us. Without him being ok with our relationship we could not move forward. We could not enjoy our love like we wanted to, like we planned and waited for so long. His anger towards me seemed to grow and grow.

Finally, she had to pick. Her son had to come first. He had to come first before when she found out she was pregnant and now again as a teenager. She had to recover their relationship. He only had a few years till he went to college and then she might not ever get a chance to do it. Kate had to go back to Johnny's. There was no other way. I understood. Johnny let her go with me once to save her and now life threw me a curveball because now I had to let her go in order to save her....again.

Today she was going over to Johnny's to talk to him about getting back with him. I don't know how all this was going to work out. I loved Kate so much I just focused on her happiness. She was all that I cared about. I needed for her to regain her son's love. Only then I could shake some of the guilt I had been carrying. I understood that it was the only way.

To my surprise after just an hour, the door opened and Kate was back. She came inside with her head down and instantly I knew things did not go well for her. My heart skipped a beat. She was back so soon. Not a good sign even though inside I was so happy to see her back her. Then I saw the tears in her eyes. I hated to see her sad eyes. I could never stand to see her cry.

"Jax, he does not believe me. I told him I wanted to come back home. I wanted for us to be a family again. I told him I could not stand doing this to Xander. I asked him, no I begged him for a chance and he said no! What am I going to do now?"

"Kate, you will go back tomorrow and say the same thing. No man that truly loves you will be able to resist you. One thing I can say about Johnny even though I hate to say this is that he does love you. I see it in his eyes every time we are all together. I can promise you that eventually he will summit. I also hate to admit but he has always proven to be a good man and a good friend to you especially helping you with Xander all these years. He has never had another serious love interest since you left him. I'm telling you he loves you. Try again."

Did I just spit out those words? They hurt me to the core of my bones to say them. I was telling the love of my life to go to another man and beg for him to take her back. In what universe was this normal? If Kate only knew how this tore me up inside. Here I was helping my rival to accept the love of my life back into his home and into his life.

How could Johnny say no to Kate? Even for a minute. Kate was an angel. How can he resist being near her and smelling her sweet smell? Touching her soft skin was heaven. I would have jumped at the chance if I was him. It kind of angered me to even think about it. I hated that Kate had to go and lower herself to have to even ask Johnny to take her back. But then again, I could imagine he did not want to be hurt again and he probably saw through Kate's true purpose and knew she did it out of love for Xander and not really for him.

The next day Kate decided to go back and try again. Every time she left the house I felt I would lose her forever. I told myself ok this is it. The end of us. This time she did not come back. I lost her. Oh God, she was gone. She was truly gone this time.

He had to have said yes. Was she in his arms? He had to be feeling like the luckiest guy in the world. He had her back. I was lost. I had to hold myself back from running to get her and begging her to come back to me that all of this had been a mistake. How could I live without her after having lived with her for so long? I sat there and had to talk myself out of doing this.

I looked around our apartment and she was everywhere. She was in the coffeepot she picked out and was so excited to have. She was in pillows the that she bought for our sofa, she was in the curtains, she was in the bedroom, she was everywhere. She still had to come back for her stuff and for Xander's stuff so all her clothes hung in the closet.

I could smell her in our home. I had asked her to call me before she came so I could make sure not to be here because I could not bear it. As soon as she got her stuff I would move to a new apartment. I could not be here where we shared so many memories, we shared a bed, we shared a life, we shared our hearts.

I paced around the apartment that night feeling restless. I let her go but I could not even see my future without her in it? Who would be here to greet me when I got home? Who would I reach over at night to spoon with? Who would laugh at my stupid jokes? I could not believe that she would not be walking back through that door tonight. I would not be rolling towards her in the middle of the night and feeling her next to me.

I had nobody except Kate. Kate was my whole family. Kate was my whole world. What was left for me? Should I go back to Avian? Should I stay here? She was the reason I came to this planet in the first place. I lost my way. I had no purpose any more. For the first time in a long time I was lost. Johnny had everything. I had nothing. Why did one of us have to lose for the other to win?

Then the phone rang. Who could possibly be calling now? I ran to the phone.

"Hello?"

"Hi, it's me."

Her voice. I wanted to reach through the phone lines and kiss her. My heart stood still. Was she coming back?

"I just wanted for you to know that I'm ok. Johnny said he would give it a try. He still feels confused and scared of getting hurt again but he said it was best for Xander so he could not refuse."

"Oh, I'm glad. I think it is for the best. " What else could I say?

"Jax, are you going to be ok?"

How was I supposed to answer that?

"No, not for a long time but if you ever need me, if you ever need me for anything Kate look for me. I will be here in the shadows, in the background….again. I think this is the place that I was always meant for. "

"Jax, thank you for loving me this way. Maybe one day, in another lifetime we will make our way back to Avian. To the place, we were the happiest. Take care of yourself. I love you."

The next sound I heard was the noise of the dial tone. It was done. The tears ran down my face. This was Kate's way of saying good bye. She needed some type of closing to our chapter and I was done. I remembered everything we had gone through. Why? What was the purpose of everything? I felt so angry with the elders, with God and with myself. As much as I tried I always failed. The world had failed us.

I got up the next day and left in search of a new home. I need a fresh start to be able to start to recover. I found a little town home not far away. I signed the contract and moved in right away. Here I was starting over again. The story repeated itself but with each new beginning I lost a piece of myself and this time I lost the biggest, most important part which was Kate.

24 REUNITED

Johnny brought me in to his home because I know considered it his home. It would never feel like "our" home again. I hired someone to get my stuff along with Xanders because I could not go back to my real home. That small apartment where I shared so many moments with Jax. Moments that were over but that would stay with me forever. I was grateful for those few years we had together.

Xander took it just like I expected. He was over the moon with happiness. He came and hugged Johnny and I when we told him. I had not seen him this happy since he was a little boy. This was the reason I did all of this. This exact moment is what gave me the strength to continue. My son, I thought to myself if you could only imagine what I had just done for you. What I had to give up because of my love for you. If you ever knew you would never again doubt how much I feel for you.

From then on Xander became a role model of a son. His grades were up, his behavior was excellent. He smiled all of the time and he was finally happy. The days passed by. Johnny was not sure how to act when I came back to the house. We slept in the same bed but all we did was sleep. He did not touch me. I slept on my side of the bed and he slept on his side. Which was a good think because I don't know how I could have lived with him being intimate with me again.

During the day, we talked just like we use to about our current jobs, about Xander and normal routine everyday stuff. If felt nice to have his friendship in my life again. I had missed these talks with him. I never stopped caring for him as a friend. We started to build our friendship again. I admired him as a person. He was hardworking, loyal, caring and very intelligent. He never raised his voice or let his temper get the best of him. Actually, Jax had the same qualities. They were both really similar. If it had been different circumstances they could have been good friends.

Jax. The things Jax was willing to do for me showed me that he was like no-one else. I usually would go to the park because that was just our place. I liked to think about him. I felt him there. I always looked for him. I waited for him to one day appear to me again. Sometimes I thought I watched a glimpse of him. I never told Johnny of these escapes. I waited and waited till the day he would by miracle show up and then one day he did.

"Hi."

I was in shock, so much that I could not even answer!

"How are you? How are things with Xander?"

"They are good. Xander is doing great."

"I'm glad then. You have your son again." He smiled but his face looked so sad. I was scared to go up to him. I felt that I did not deserve him. I made him suffer so much.

"I'm sorry Jax. I miss you."

"I miss you too. I actually came here today to say good bye."

"What? Good bye? Are you going back to Avian?"

"Maybe. I just need to let you go. I can't go on like this. I'm a mess."

"I understand. I can't hold you here"

I wanted to tell him not to go, not to leave me but how could I? I could not offer him anything right now. What could I say? What could I do? I could not continue to be so selfish with him. He was alone while I at least had a family and a home.

"Can I hug you?" I asked.

He stepped towards me and we held on to each other and cried together. And just like that that was that. Our love story was coming to an end. My boy was leaving me.

As I walked away that day I decided not to return to the park. I had to let him go and not keep holding him back. I saw how destroyed he looked. I destroyed his life and his hopes. He came to this world searching for love and would leave feeling more alone than ever. I could not give him the love that I had inside that only he was able to receive. What would we do with all this love? Would he find someone else to give it to?

Time kept passing, days turned to weeks, weeks turned to months, months to years. I never saw Jax again. I worried. I had not felt his presence like I had in the past. He just vanished. I wondered if he ended up going to Avian. The thought of it scared me. Even if he was so far from me at least I knew we were in the same planet. I know this had to be hard on him. How many times he had stepped aside because of me. I just pictured him alone somewhere knowing I was here with Johnny. I missed him dearly.

I wished I could see him and talk to him. I wanted to tell him about my situation. I wanted him to know that we were together but not really together. We had converted to being like friends, like roommates but we haven't been together, together like man and woman or a husband and wife. We had not had any relations at all. Which was a relief for me because after Jax there was no-one else for me. He wasn't the type of man to force it on me and I could tell he definitely knew I was not ready up for that. Maybe if I could tell Jax all these things he would feel better or maybe I was just being selfish again and telling him everything was just to make myself feel better.

I had to find him just to know that he was fine. After that I could continue to live this life. I don't know if I had persuaded myself just to give myself a reason to look for him or not but I knew I had to try. I had two possible places to find him. His job at the adoption agency if he still worked there or the park which I had not returned to since that last day we said goodbye to each other the last time. Everywhere else it would be just pure luck to run into him. I had to try. It had been years since I last saw him and it was time.

I first went to his job and found out he had resigned and took another job offer shortly after we broke up. They did not know where he had gone. I went to the park a few times but also had no luck. I sat at a coffee shop that we use to come to. Where were you Jax? Where are you? All of a sudden there he was. I saw him.

He was walking towards a town home nearby. He opened the door and disappeared inside. This must be his home. I quickly paid my tab and ran over there. I would always wonder it this was just dumb luck or fate. At that point I didn't care. All I cared about was him. My boy. My blonde, blue eyed boy.

I knocked on the door and no answer. Knocked again still nothing. I started to bang harder and harder. I was not going to go anywhere until he opened the door. I saw him and knew he was here. Finally, the door opened. I let myself in and I took a good look at him. Except he didn't look like himself. He looked like he had not shaved in a long time. His hair was long pulled back in a ponytail. He was dressed raggedy looking. This was not Jax's style at all in fact quite the opposite of how he maintained his image. He had always dressed and maintained himself like a true Avian. Clean cut, shaved, dressed in fitted, light clothes and smelling good. Where was my beautiful boy?

"Oh Jax. What happened to you?"

"Kate, why are you here?"

"I was looking for you. I went to your job and they told me you took another job. I looked for you at the park. I needed to see you!"

"Kate, I can't do this. I can't. You are with Johnny now and I can't be with you. This life. The heart breaks. I just can't."

"Jax, I just need to tell you that ...."

"Stop. Kate whatever it is you are going to tell me just don't. I can't do this. Please you have to let me go. I did"

"But Jax,,,,don't you love me anymore? Did these years wipe out our love? Did you find a new love? Is that it? You've never pushed me away before? You don't know."

"Kate these years without you have been hell. I could not seek you out, I could not fight for you I could not do anything without hurting your son and that I would not take any risk doing. Do you have any idea what that was like for me?"

"The thought of you in Johnny's arms, in his bed, with him everyday kills me. I can't play this game anymore. I wiped you out of my life but never out of my heart. Now you show up here and I have to see you again and for what? To lose you again and go through the agony of letting you go?"

"Jax I just have to tell you I am with Johnny but not in the way you think. Since I went back with him he has never touched me. He has respected me always. I have not been with anyone since you! I thought eventually maybe I would have to. But everything is different. Johnny accepted the fact that he is just a friend years ago. He knows I love you and have always loved you."

I moved to get closer to Jax. Quickly he stopped me.

"Please don't come closer. I won't be able to contain myself. Please."

I then grabbed him and started to passionately kiss him. I kissed him on his neck, his mouth and he then grabbed me and kissed me back so hard. Like he could not breath without me. I did not care about the consequences. I could not stop myself any longer. My body longed for him and his for me. We both knew we would not be able to stop. We made love and connected just like we always did. It was as natural as breathing air.

That day I was the one that brought Jax back to life.

25 THE GIRL

"What are we going to do now?" I asked Jax still at his townhouse.

"I don't know about you but I have to go clean myself up!" he laughed at himself to make a joke out of the situation. "Geesh, I'm a complete mess. You see what living without you does to me!"

"Ok, go bring back the Jax I really know. I want him back."

A few moments later, he came back to the room.

"There he is! My boy, now that is the boy I came looking for. Now come here and kiss me you big alien, you."

We kissed for what seemed to be forever. I did not want to stop but there were things I had to do now. It was time to clean up not just ourselves but our lives.

"I have to go now but now I know where to find you! Believe me I will be back you won't be able to get rid of me anymore" I joked back.

"You promise? Next time you come over we will sit and figure this out. Together we can think of something and if we don't I am sure we can figure out what to do with our time together!"

If was as if Jax's spirit had returned to his body. He now looked refreshed, ready to go conquer the world or at least our love. I don't know what would have happened if I would have never showed up looking for him.

Ok then I started to head on out. "Oh and Kate...."
"Yeah?"
"What took you so long!"

"Hey if I had to go to another universe to drag you back here I was going to, like I said I know where you live and where you're really from!" I winked.

That afternoon Xander got home from school and sat down for dinner. Johnny was in the office working on revealing some photographs for an important project he was working on.

"Xander, can I ask you something?" I was scared to bring Jax up again but I had to try. I looked at him and thought how much he had changed these past years.

"Yeah mom, anything."

"I want to ask you something, just don't get angry. It's just a question. Can you tell me why you hated Jax so much?"

"Mom, I'm older now. I'm now sixteen years old. You can ask me whatever you want even if it is about Jax. I haven't thought about him for years. I guess I was so mad at him for you leaving dad. I blamed him and at the same time I was a little jealous. I'm sorry for what I put you through. I do have to admit I am glad he just left. I figure it was because of me but I have to be honest and admit that he made me happy by leaving you."

"Xander, I understand why you felt like that. I know that you were young and did not understand everything that was happening. Maybe it was my fault because I made you go through a lot of changes too fast. I love you. I just want you to know that."

"I love you too mom and I'm sorry for the suffering that I put you through. Thank you for picking me over him." He looked back at me a little confused.

I decided to leave it at that. While he wasn't a little boy anymore he was a teenager and I did not want to risk him becoming that angry kid he used to be. I did not have the solution. I wanted to explain to him how much I loved him and how he was everything to me. I wanted to tell him that Jax was the love of my life but I was scared. Deep inside I still felt the hurt that I went through. Xander would find out that I indeed cheated on his dad and how would he feel about that. He would probably never forgive me. Johnny was such a good husband I could not defend myself. It would have been different if Johnny was a drunk, a cheater or an abuser but he wasn't. He had always been a wonderful father and husband. I did not blame Xander for always defending and protecting his father so much. Johnny deserved so much more than what I was able to give to him. We continued to be friends throughout the years. Johnny understood that I could never again be with him and he accepted me like that. He was a remarkable human being. I had not able to make Jax happy or Johnny happy!

.....Xander......

I woke up today and did not understand why my mom brought up Jax yesterday. He was in the past. I wanted to tell her that I actually feel really bad for the way I behaved and that Jax was actually a good guy. I knew that she loved him. With dad, she was never the same. She did not look at him or treat him the way she did with Jax. I just did not want to say anything or admit it to my mom because the selfish part of me wanted my parents to stay together even if I knew they were more like friends than husband and wife.

I got dressed, ate my breakfast and then looked at my mom as she was washing the dishes. I walked over to her and hugged her from behind. I loved her so much. I knew she came back with dad because of me. My mother was so good to me.

"What was that for!"

"Mom, I just want to say I love you."

"Ok, not complaining, I love you too!"

"Ok I'm off to school then, see you later mom."

"Ok love take care."

I grabbed my jacket, grabbed my backpack and was ready to face another day. I opened the front door, looked up and there across the street was the most beautiful girl in the world. Long blonde hair, big green eyes kind of like my own. She stared at me, I stared back. I think I fell in love. I stood there struck by her beauty and all of a sudden, she was gone!

That evening when I got home I told my mom about it. She started to tear up.

"Mom, are you going to cry because I like a girl?"

"No Xander, I think you are old enough for me to tell you my story. My story with......Jax."

"What! Why? What does he have to do with me liking a girl?
"

"Nothing and everything. Please hear me out without hating me. I might be able to help you with this girl."

"But you don't even know her? I don't even know her."

"I do."

I sat there with my son that day and told him my love story about that boy. When I was done. We were crying together.

"Oh, my gosh mom what did I do? I broke you guys apart. I didn't know. I'm sorry."

"No, you didn't because true soulmates always find their way back to each other. They are always connected. I don't know this girl but if you feel what I just described because I felt it from the very first second. I can tell you what you need to do. Next time you see her run to her, grab her hand and never let her go. Don't waste any time Learn from my mistakes."

26 LOVE

Her name was Bianca. Xander and Bianca were now officially a couple. They were inseparable. I had learned to love her like the daughter I never had. It was a little tough for Johnny. He was having a little rough time seeing them together. That was not good. I had to talk to him. I had to explain to him that they needed to be together. My son deserved to be happy. I needed for him to be happy.

"Johnny dear can I speak to you in private please?"

"Yeah, sure lets go up to the bedroom and talk."

Xander and Bianca were watching movies on the couch being happy just like teenagers did when they were dating. We went to the room and sat on the bed. I looked up and saw a dear friend sitting in front of me. I took my hand and caressed his face.

"Oh, Johnny I'm sorry I was never able to make you happy like you deserved. So sorry."

"It wasn't your fault, you don't control who your soulmate will be. Isn't that the way it goes? One look and your hooked. Just like Xander and Bianca?"

"Johnny, you have to be happy for them. They are in love and with our support they can get their happily ever after. Why can't you see that?"

"Kate." Johnny's words trembled a little. "The reason that it is so hard for me is because I am seeing Jax and you every time I see them. I look at how they love each other and it is so perfect. I know see how you and Jax were. I stood in between you guys. I never wanted to. I loved you, I still love you. I go to sleep every night next to you not able to be with you and loving you so much."

"Oh Johnny…" I cried. "I know. I wish I could. What can I say? I never wanted to hurt you. You are my best friend. I don't regret having you in my life. You gave me Xander."

"I know. I know but I hurt you by keeping you next to me. I know I have to let you go. You need to be with him. I want to see you as happy as Xander is. You need to find him and finally live your life for good."

We hugged for a long time. How did I get so lucky? Two wonderful guys in my life but so unlucky to always be hurting one of them. I knew that Johnny and me were done with again, this time for good. I just had to tell Xander. I walked back to the living room saw Xander and Bianca laughing and went to the kitchen table and just sat there for a minute.

"Mom."

"Yes, sweetie?"

"Can we have a talk too?"

"Sure. Tell me what's on your mind?"

"Mom, I love Bianca so much. I don't know what I would do without her and because of me you are without Jax. You need to find him, you need to be with him. I understand that now. I think dad knows too."

The next day we went to Jax's townhouse. When he opened the door and saw Xander with me his jaw dropped to the ground.

"Xander, Kate! Come on in."

"Jax." Xander said "I am here to apologize to you. Years ago, I took mom away from you and I am here today to bring her back. She belongs with you. I hope you can forgive me. I was wrong. I acted like a brat."

"Xander, of course! I can't believe I am hearing these words from you! I tried, I really tried to win you over. Can I give you a hug?"

To watch them hug was a dream come true.

From then on everything changed. I started living again. I ended up moving to Jax's town home where I belonged. Xander and Bianca eventually graduated and were planning to go off to college together. And Johnny...well Johnny was now dating again. He met a really nice lady that happened to be related to Bianca. When she introduced them they hit it off right away. We were finally one big happy family. Jax and Johnny actually became closer and even after everything that happened learned to accept and respect each other and here we are today. It is Xander"s birthday and we are all united at Johnny's house. We all sit around the table eating together as a family.

I step outside to the backyard to get some fresh air. All of a sudden I feel Jax's arms hug me from behind.

"Do you remember!" I exclaim "It was right here we stood all those years ago!"

You were a part of another world back then. Now you belong here with me. You are a part of this family, in this home! That sweet baby that you held here so long ago loves you like a stepdad. Even Jax, our dog loved you the instant he saw you! Now there is one more person that will love you so much as well.

"Yeah who?"

"Well, that's for you to tell me. That person is right here" I told him as I placed his hands on my tummy. "What do you say boy or girl?"

Jax jumped up and that moment could not have been any more perfect. His eyes teared up with happiness.

"I finally have a family. I belong somewhere. You had said in Avian that you belong there but I think as long as we are together we will belong to each other and home will be wherever we can be like this! Annnndddd it's a little girl!!!!"

"I love you my blonde, eyed boy."

"I love you my darling, Kate"

Finally, after what seemed like a lifetime we could finally be together and nothing could tear us apart. Our future looked brighter than ever and especially with this little bundle that would come to the home with a couple that would show her what real loved was all about. If you are one of the lucky ones out there you know what I am talking about!!! wink wink.

THE END.